# KING OF MALICE

## DARK MAFIA STEAMY ROMANCE

KINGS OF LAS VEGAS

TAMMY ANDRESEN

❀ Created with Vellum

# KING OF MALICE

**King of Malice**
Kings of Las Vegas

Tammy Andresen

**I accidentally entered THE GAME.**

My best friend has disappeared.

Growing up in foster care together, she's my family, and the person who saved me on the worst day of my life.

That day is the reason I completely panic when a man touches me.

But that doesn't matter now.

It's my turn to save her.

The last place she was seen?

**A Bratva King's whorehouse.**

Dimitri Ivanov is the stuff of nightmares and completely untouchable.

Until he comes to the temp agency where I work.

**He's a single dad who needs a nanny.**

I beg, borrow, and steal to get the job. I don't care about the danger.

This is my only chance to find Cassie.

But stepping into his world is like a trial by fire…testing my strength, pushing on my every fear.

And when I'm thrust into the very GAME that has stolen my best friend, the truth becomes clear:

**Dimitri is the only man who can protect me.**

**And the last man I should trust.**

# PROLOGUE

Ava

"Now I lay me down to sleep," I softly whisper so that I can't be heard more than a few feet away. Cadence and I are pretending to be asleep, despite the raging fight happening between our foster parents just outside our door.

At fourteen, we're way too old for this kind of kiddie prayer, but the air is charged with danger, and I just need to do something.

"You never fucking shut up, woman," Al, our foster father, screams at the top of his lungs. "I'm so fucking sick of you and your stupid ideas."

"I pray the lord my soul to keep," Cadence says back, our hands reaching across the narrow space between our twin beds.

Al is a mean drunk. We know the kind. Cadence and I have been in four different foster homes in the last two years. Two together and two apart. "And if I die before I wake," I add drawing in a shaky breath.

"I pray the lord my soul to take," Cadence finishes, her eyes closing as a single tear leaks from her eye.

I tried to tell her not to put that petroleum jelly into Al's slippers. Al and Judy are two of the few foster parents who would take us together. What's more, even though Al yells a lot, he wasn't like my last foster dad who touched me whenever he could, giving me the creeps. I'll take Al any day.

But Cadence has always pushed buttons, and she hit one today. Coupled with the fact that Al came home drunk, he's ready to fight, and he definitely wants us gone.

As if to voice my thought, he screams, "I want them fucking out."

"But the money they bring in," Judy answers back in a whining tone that sounds small and weak in comparison.

"You can keep Ava, she's not a fucking problem. But Cadence..." I hear his slippers hit the wall as he throws them. "That little shit has got to go."

I squeeze Cadence's hand tighter as the door flies open and we let go of each other, me emitting a squeaking scream, as I huddle under the covers.

Cadence and I met at a group home, where, at the time, we were the two youngest kids. My mom had just died and hers might as well be dead, she's always strung out and hiding out in some crack house—that's what Cadence says.

We stuck together because the older girls were mean, and twice, when they stole my stuff, it was Cadence who snatched it back for me. One of those items was my mother's locket, the only thing I have left of her.

I've got it around my neck now.

Al stands in the doorway, backlit by the hall light. "Get your fucking stuff girl."

"It's the middle of the night, Al!" Judy cries, appearing behind him.

He turns, raising his hand. A crack sounds through the air as it comes down across Judy's cheek. His backhand is hard enough to send her crashing into the far wall. Cadence screams and scrambles from her bed, into mine, hiding behind me as Al stalks into the room.

Tears are rolling down my cheeks now too as I flop over and then roll in a ball around Cadence. I squeeze my eyes shut, like closed eyes will keep the impending hit from happening.

Al grabs me by the scruff of the neck and yanks. My head snaps and for a second, I think it might break. Pain radiates through my head and back as I scream out in pain and fear.

But he doesn't snap my neck. Instead, I fly through the air, landing on Cadence's bed with a bounce.

He leans down over Cadence, smacking the back of her head hard. "You think that was fucking funny," he screams an inch from her face, her hands wrapped around her head, her knees drawn up to her chest as she tries to protect herself.

But she doesn't cave. She's disadvantaged in every way, but she still fights. "It was hilarious," Cadence screeches back instead.

"Cadence," I gasp, trying to help her see reason.

I hear the next hit, the force of Al's hand ringing through the room.

"Al," I cry next, but I'm frozen in fear, not able to move as he hits her a third time.

"Get your stuff and get the fuck out," he says in her face but she's not moving now. She's so still, that fear beats in my chest like a drum, pulsing all the way up to my ears.

"Cadence," I half whisper, half sob. "Cadence."

He spins on me, his face twisted in rage. "Shut the fuck up or you'll be next."

I shrink back down in her bed as Al storms from the room and slams the door behind him. I wait for a second, two, to make sure he doesn't come back in the room. Then I'm off the bed. "Cadence?"

She gives a low moan and a little of the tension in my chest unwinds. I jump back on my bed, wrapping her in my arms. "Oh Cadence, tell me you're all right."

"Someday, I'll make him pay," she says, blood dripping from the corner of her mouth.

I squeeze her tightly. I wish she wouldn't bait our foster fathers like that. It's going to be so difficult to get put in another place together. Maybe I can beg Al tomorrow to let us stay. But it's probably too late.

If we have to leave, we have to leave. Cadence is my only family now, and where she goes, I go.

I push up, trying to assess her bruises in the dark. "I'm sorry I couldn't stop him—"

She grimaces, turning over, away from me. "You're a good girl, Ava. It's not your style."

My heart seizes in my chest. Does she wish I'd fight for us more? Guilt makes me curl away. "I'd do anything for you."

She doesn't answer as she wipes more of the blood dripping down her chin.

# CHAPTER ONE

Ava

I step off the bus, the stop only a block from my office building, and pull my phone from my purse.

Dialing the phone, I huff a breath of impatience even as I straighten my skirt, striding down the crowded Vegas thoroughfare. This time of day, the tourists aren't clogging up the sidewalks as much as the army of workers coming off a night of work, or the ones starting the day-shift. But either way, they hustle, jostling each other and me as they pass.

I can't bother with the irritation, my attention on willing Cadence to finally pick up her phone.

The line rings several times before it goes to voicemail. My eye close for a split second, my fingers touching the locket around my neck. "Cadence," I beg into the phone. "It's been days. Where are you? Call me…" I hesitate. "I'm worried."

I frown as I hang up, rubbing the worn locket between my fingers. It's not the first time Cadence has gone missing. I should be better at controlling the panic by now.

She usually resurfaces after an epic binge of some kind or another.

But I thought those days had passed. That she'd cleaned up and was ready to live a straight, healthy life. She'd taken a job as a receptionist at a small company that I placed her in myself.

Then again, I'm pretty sure she and her latest boyfriend had an epic breakup, which never fails to send her on a path to self-destruction.

Frowning, I enter the lobby of my office, the air conditioning instantly cooling my skin.

At twenty-five, I've been working here since I was nineteen when I first applied to be one of the temps. I impressed the intake officer enough to get referred to HR, where I did a short stint in the nanny department before I was placed on staff instead.

I managed to get a college degree at night, while working full-time, while I also worked my way up the ranks at one of the largest agencies in the country.

Another city probably wouldn't support a temp agency of this size, but in Vegas, temporary positions are big business.

With the number of workers needed to run the tourist industry, every company, big or small, uses us for staffing.

I run one of our smallest departments, nannies. My boss has hinted about giving me a bigger sector, but I'm happy with the work I do and don't want to change.

Placing hired nannies with the right family is a job for which I feel intimately acquainted, and I work tirelessly to get it right. And while technically we're a temp agency, the percentage of employees who take on permanent positions from our placements is amazingly high.

So, every placement is done with care, and I place all nannies with the expectation they'll stay in their positions.

I smile at the receptionists and make my way up the elevator, bypassing the kitchen on my floor, to make my way straight to my desk.

Setting my bag with my lunch on the surface, I pick up my work phone, dialing the small insurance company where I placed Cadence six months ago.

"Bright Side Insurance," a receptionist, who is not Cadence, answers.

"Hi, this is Ava Tantor from Temps For You. I'm calling to speak with Walter, please."

"Mister Cartwright? He's not in yet. Can I take a message?"

"Please." I give her my information and then I take a quick breath. "But also, we placed the last girl in your position. Cadence."

"Oh yeah. I heard about her. Left suddenly…"

My heart starts to pound in my chest. "Any idea where she went?"

"No." the girl on the other end of the phone sounds skeptical, like it's weird that I'm asking. "Why?"

I clear my throat. "She left incomplete paperwork here at the temp agency," I quickly cover. "Trying to track her down."

"Oh," she sounds relieved. "Right. All I know is she came in last week and said she needed three weeks off. Mister Cartwright refused so she quit and then he hired me. I'm his niece."

Shit. Shit. Shit. "Thank you so much. And if you could, please give him the message I called." I hang up, the knot in my stomach so tight I feel like I might be sick.

Picking up the phone, I dial another number I know by heart.

"Steve Imperian, investigator for hire."

Steve is a guy we use here at work pretty regularly. If a temp files a complaint against an employer, we do our due diligence to find out who is actually at fault before we proceed.

But I've used him privately to track Cadence on a couple of occasions.

I make good money for my age, and I live pretty simply. Small apartment, no car, thrift my clothes when I can.

I save half of my income every month in order to protect myself from any kind of disaster.

But on more than one occasion, I've used that money to bail out Cadence. From hiring investigators, to paying off some drug dealer she'd gotten herself in deep with, to sending her to rehab that she didn't have the insurance to cover.

She hates it when I spend my money on her, so I try not to offer unless the situation is really bad. Cadence sees my help as a red line under her personal failures, I think, but it's not true. I'm not trying to highlight her mistakes, just ease her suffering.

She's my only family, and she had it way tougher than me. But also, and we both know this, if shit were really going down, Cadence is the one who'd save my ass. We're a team.

"Hey Steve, it's Ava from Temps For You."

"Hey, gorgeous, good to hear from you. How's it going? Did you change your mind about having dinner with me?"

"I'll get back to you on dinner," I answer, my voice laced with the tension I'm barely able to hold in. "I've got a problem that I'm hoping you can help me with."

"Cadence again?" I hear his chair squeak as he sits up. "What is it this time?"

With a sigh, I tell him the little I know.

He listens silently, hearing everything I've got to say before he taps his finger on his desk. "Honestly, I wouldn't worry too much."

"You think?"

"I'll look into it for sure, I'd do anything for you, and you know I'll get you answers, but hear me out. If she asked for time off, planned something in advance, she's fine."

His words really do make me feel better and the knot in my stomach unwinds. "You're right. Maybe she just fell in with a group who decided to tour the country on a bus, or is taking a trip to Ibiza, or…" I trail off as I try to think of another adventure she hasn't been on that could take a month. "Gone on safari?"

Steve laughs. "I'll get you answers. Same rate as always."

"Thanks, Steve."

I'm about to hang up when I hear him hesitate. "Ava."

My mouth twitches as I wait for what's coming. Hopefully not another dinner invitation. Steve's cute enough but I'm just… "Yeah?"

"Are you sure you want to do this? Track her down? I know it's not my business, but she puts you through hell…"

I bite my tongue, wanting to tell him he's right, it's none of his business. I'm not paying him for advice. I draw in a slow breath of air through my nose and then let it out. "She's my sister, Steve. The only one I've got."

"All right," he says in a voice that makes it clear he's shaking his head. "I'll get back to you as soon as I can."

"Thanks." I hang up, relieved I'll have answers soon. The nice thing about giving him so much work is he'll be quick. Temps For Us is a priority customer.

I'm about to return to the kitchen to put my lunch in the fridge and get started with my day, when my phone rings.

Stopping, I pick it up. "Temps For You, this is Ava, how may I help you?"

"Ava," A man says on the other side of the line with the kind of deep baritone that moves through me like a shiver. "What a beautiful name."

I've heard that line a million times, but it's the first time that it makes me feel something other than irritation. A warmth slides through my stomach settling between my legs.

I don't date. I've tried a couple of times, but it doesn't really work for me. I can't relax enough to enjoy myself.

But this man, with his eastern European accent and his honey-rich voice has my heart skipping a beat, wondering why I don't give it another try.

"Thank you. Very kind. Who do I have the pleasure of speaking with?"

"Dimitri Ivanov."

"Mister Ivanov—"

"Call me, Dimitri."

"Dimitri," the name slides off my tongue as it dances over the back of my teeth. "How can I help you?"

"I'm hoping to hire a nanny."

I find myself biting my lip before I answer. "In that case, you've called the right person."

He laughs, warm and low, and the ache between my legs actually throbs. "Excellent."

"I'd like to collect some information, Dimitri, and then I can schedule a visit to your home to complete the intake interview."

"How long will all this take? I'm in a bind with my daughter and her care."

"I can send someone as early as tomorrow or the next day for short-term care, but if you're looking for someone you hope might take the position permanently, the more time I take with the placement, the more likely the pairing will be successful."

He pauses for a moment. "A short-term option would be most helpful. And we can proceed with your plan for a long-term solution. But I'm a quick decision maker myself, and if I could meet the candidates, I'd quickly know which would suit my family."

My lips purse. I take pride in being good at my job. In addition, when clients choose incorrectly, they very much forget they are actually to blame. "A possibility we can discuss when we meet." I flip open my calendar. "I've got a spot open at three-thirty this afternoon if you'd like to move forward with the intake?"

"That sounds excellent. Thank you."

"You're welcome, Dimitri, I'll see you then." I shift, wondering if he looks half as delicious as he sounds.

He makes this masculine rumble in his throat that has me pulsing all over again. "I look forward to it, Ava. This afternoon."

The line goes dead. But it's at least a minute before I place the receiver back in its cradle and start for the kitchen to finally put away my lunch. It's not even nine in the morning and this day is already crazy.

Then again, it's got all kinds of potential to turn absolutely insane.

# CHAPTER TWO

Ava

Standing on the sidewalk, I stare up at the luxury condo in a swanky downtown neighborhood, my neck craning up the six-story building. At the top is a penthouse apartment with a large balcony that is decorated in lush plants. Does the balcony have a sprinkler system? I sigh as I imagine the luxuries money brings.

I'm happy with my choices, to save instead of spending my salary, but sometimes…

I know I'm stalling.

I should have gone straight inside, but I'm nervous to meet the man with the voice that wreaked havoc on my body all morning.

Every time I thought of the sound of his honey baritone, I got warm all over again.

Now is not the time for these kinds of feelings. Even if Cadence hadn't just disappeared again, I'm finally comfortable living this life on my own. I've stopped wanting a man, stopped wishing I could be a normal girl with regular reactions to sex. I'm just going to be weirdo me.

Which is why I straighten my spine and hike my messenger bag strap further up my shoulder before I cross the street and enter the building.

Which has a concierge…

"Dimitri Ivanov, please," I ask with a smile, staring at the uniformed man in a cap and gloves.

"Name?" he asks with a generic smile back.

"Ava Tantor."

"He's expecting you, Ms. Tantor." And then the concierge steps around his counter height desk and waves for me to follow him to an elevator separate from the bank of elevators at the back of the lobby.

He inserts a key, the doors sliding open, as he sweeps his hand, inviting me into the interior. My brows are halfway up my forehead. The man with the honey baritone has a private elevator that can only be operated with a key.

I just know I'm headed up to the penthouse.

Sure enough, there is only one button in the elevator, the letter P emblazoned on it.

I push the button as the doors close, the elevator whizzing up to the top floor. I've never been in one that went this fast.

The doors open before I've even processed, and I can barely keep from gasping as the interior of the apartment appears.

I'm in a stunning entry with marble floors, beautiful artwork displayed on walls that must be at least twelve feet tall.

From a room I can't see, the most beautiful classical piano music fills the space. The speakers in this place must be amazing.

Tentatively, I step out of the elevator, examining one of the pieces to the right. A landscape that I think might be an actual Monet.

"Hello?" I call, taking another step into the hall.

The piano music abruptly stops as I realize, it wasn't a recording I was hearing but an actual person playing.

"Hello," that honey baritone calls. "Please come in, Ava."

And then footsteps approach.

In what feels like slow motion, I turn my head to the man walking toward me. Dear lord above, I'm in trouble.

He's ridiculously tall, his shoulders so broad, he seems to fill the large entry. He has the sort of sharp, masculine good looks that are both refined and rugged, his dark hair sweeps back from his high forehead. He's older than me, a touch of gray at his temples. But it makes him look even more handsome. Distinguished. Powerful.

Maybe it's the confidence with which he carries himself.

He's breathtaking and I've lost the ability to speak. "Hi," I finally push out, sounding more like a schoolgirl than the professional woman I've become. I've already said hello. "Thank you."

I chastise myself and then step forward, holding out my hand in an attempt to recover myself. "Pleased to meet you in person, Dimitri."

"And you, Ava," he takes my hand, his easily twice the size of mine as his skin glides along my palm. It sends an absolute riot of sensation through my body, as I try to hold myself together.

I'm not equipped for this. I have no point of reference for an attraction this strong. Or really any attraction at all.

I try to make my brain work again as he keeps my hand in his, a small smile playing at his lips.

Can he tell how I feel? The way he's affecting me? I try to shake it off even as his other hand comes to the outside of mine, my little hand completely engulfed in both of his. I resist the urge to fiddle with my hair as my cheeks heat.

But that's when I notice. His hands…

They're covered in sinister tattoos. I blink at them, trying to decide what they mean.

"Umm," I say before I can stop myself, fumbling from both confusion and attraction. I don't do this. I take situations head on with a professional demeanor that makes people forget I'm still too young to be head of a department, and I put them at ease. "I'm hoping to ask you a few questions to help get your search for a nanny started."

"I look forward to answering them. Let's have a seat in the living room. Can I get you something to drink?"

"I'm good, thank you."

He finally lets go of my hand and leads the way past a stunning, top of the line, kitchen and into a large living room with oversized leather furniture.

Sure enough, in one corner is a baby grand piano. The kind I've only seen in hotel bars. The windows behind it offer a stunning view of the Las Vegas skyline.

He gestures for me to sit on one sofa as he takes a seat in the other across from me.

That's when a little girl toddles in from the hallway that must lead to the back of the apartment. She looks to be about three, with her dark hair in a high ponytail and her big brown eyes the picture of innocence.

I give her a smile and a small wave. She doesn't wave back. "Who dat?" She points at me, her lips pulling into a tiny little adorable frown.

Dimitri gets up and crosses the room to pick her up in his arms. "That is Ms. Tantor."

"Ava," I say, returning to standing. "I'm so happy to meet you…"

"Anastasia," he fills in for me. "But I call her Anna."

"And how old are you, Anna?"

She stares at me, ducking her head under Dimitri's chin. "Tell Miss Ava how old you are," he softly encourages. I like it. He's encouraging independence without any sharp note of judgment.

"Free," she answers, curling deeper into Dimitri.

"What a big girl," I gush, my smile growing. "Is she your only child?"

"Yes."

I clear my throat, this next question is always delicate. "Marital status?"

"Widowed."

My mouth opens as I look at the two of them, my heart breaking for both of them. "I'm so sorry for your loss."

He gives a quick nod. "One of my aunts came from Russia and stayed for close to a year, but it was time for her to return home. I've tried two other agencies, but I've not had much luck finding the right nanny."

I nod. "Despite being a temp agency, we have an excellent record of placing employees in permanent positions. I can provide you a short-term nanny only, while you search for a more a more permanent option, or I can help you find a person interested in temp to permanent."

He gives a single jerk of his chin. "I need help now, but I'd like your help finding someone permanent. Thank you."

"Not a problem." I sit again, smoothing my pencil skirt, before pulling out the intake forms from my bag. I begin entering in the information I've already discovered as Dimitri takes a seat on the couch across from me.

"What sort of hours are you looking for?"

"I work a great deal, often at odd times, so I'd like a live-in nanny."

I frown. "Those are tough to find. There are overtime regulations and—"

"The pay is of no consequence."

I'd picked up on that. "Would you be open to two different people in the role?"

"I'd strongly prefer one."

If I were less professional, or less attracted, I'd suggest he consider marrying again. What he really wants is a mother. "I'll see what I can do."

I finish up my questions, placing the forms back in my bag. "Would it be possible for me to see Anna's room?"

"Of course."

The bedroom always gives me a good idea of what the caregiving parent values.

"I can also show you the nanny's room." Dimitri stands, setting Anna down as he takes her hand and starts leading her out of the living room.

She toddles next to him, her entire hand wrapped about one of his fingers.

Honestly, it melts my heart to see it, and I have to keep a sigh from escaping my lips as my heels click on the floor behind them.

We pass a large and well-appointed dining room on the way to a hallway with several doors. He opens the first, showing me a beautiful room for a little girl, decorated in pale pinks and dark wood furniture. It's pretty, yet serviceable, with books and sensory toys that are age appropriate. The room speaks of taste, sophistication, and careful parenting. "It's a beautiful room," I say with a smile.

Dimitri nods. "Thank you. The designer made certain to work some of my furniture tastes in while ensuring it was appropriate for a little girl."

Noted. Any nanny I choose, should be sophisticated enough to blend into this house and all the support staff that come with it.

We step back out, entering the room just across the hall. It's a large room with a walk-in closet and an ensuite bath. "This will be the nanny's room."

My brows lift. This is for hired help? I briefly wonder what the main bedroom looks like. "Very nice."

"I tried to hire a woman from my home country, a friend of a friend, but it did not work out," Dimitri offers with a grimace. Anna lifts her arms to her father and Dimitri bends over to pick her up, his face coming close enough to mine that I catch a whiff of his cologne. He smells like fresh winter air and pine. I draw in a deep breath, wondering how the scent is even possible in the Vegas heat.

He swings Anna into his arms, settling her on his hip as he straightens back up.

"I'm sure we can find you and Anna a good fit." Anna holds out a hand to me, her fingers opening and closing like she's reaching out for me.

It's so sweet, my chest gets tight as I slip my thumb into her palm, her fingers wrapping around it. My fingers close as I lightly stroke the back of her velvet hand. "With a little girl this adorable, it's going to be easy as pie."

"Pie?" she asks, perking up.

I laugh, giving her fist a light shake.

My gaze drifts from Anna to Dimitri where my heart stops in my chest. The way he's looking at me, it's…

I freeze, fighting the urge to back away.

There is an aggression in his gaze that makes me want to run. Hide. I drop Anna's hand, my gaze dropping too, as I draw in a deep breath through my nose and then out my mouth, attempting to control the panic.

It's ridiculous and unprofessional. I will my voice to work, to come out of my throat sounding normal. "Let me take a look at the candidates and see who might be a match. In the meantime, I'll contact Gertrude, an older woman who does short-term placements but isn't interested in long term work. She'll be a great interim fix while we're interviewing. I should hear back from her by this evening or tomorrow at the latest."

"Thank you," he rumbles. "Your competence and professionalism have been most appreciated."

His words help me relax as I shake off my reaction and walk back out of the room. I know I'm acutely sensitive in this regard.

Another reason the nanny department works for me. I work with a lot more women than I do men.

Retrieving my bag, I wave goodbye to Anna and then draw in a deep breath as I meet Dimitri's eye.

I'm surprised when my body reacts again, the ache between my legs pulsing despite the fear I'd experienced just a minute ago.

"You'll call me and let me know about the temporary placement?"

"Of course," I nod. "Is there a time that's too late for me to phone?"

"No, any time is fine." He reaches out his hand and I only hesitate for a second before I slip my fingers into his.

There is no fear at his touch, in fact, red-hot excitement pulses through me. "I'll call you as soon as I've secured someone for the short-term position, but I'll also get started on your long-term placement."

"Excellent. Thank you, Ava." He squeezes my hand, the slight pressure making my pulse jump.

My breath catches as I fight down the attraction. This is a client, but more importantly…I don't do this—ever.

I press my lips together as I try to get my body under control, pulling my hand from his before I smooth my pencil skirt over my hip.

I dart my gaze to his just in time to note that his eyes are on my hands, following the trail.

Just this once, I wish I could put my issues aside, take him up on the offer I think I see in his eyes.

I know men find me attractive.

I've got long blonde hair, blue eyes, a nice nose and mouth, a good figure. I work at being thin, but I'm curvy by design, so I fill out a bikini.

I went to three different high schools in four years, and I'd had my pick of boyfriends. Not that I let things go too far, back then I was a little scared of the unknown and sex was some exciting, but mysterious act.

Now, though, I'm petrified of the known. The moment where a man can completely dominate you and there isn't a thing you can do about it.

That memory makes me draw in a deep, cleansing breath, filling my lungs, before I give him my bright, professional smile. "I'll be in touch."

And then I turn, even as he presses the button for the elevator, the doors sliding open as I step inside.

It isn't until the doors close, that I release the breath. And make a note. I have to do as few home visits with Dimitri Ivanov as possible.

I've tried this before. Where I meet a man I decide I want to date. I mean, I've never felt the pull like I do with Dimitri, but still, I have attempted dating.

The two other times I've felt an attraction the night ended the same. Me freaking out in the bedroom once clothes started coming off and his body climbed on top of mine.

I just don't want to see the disappointment in his eyes when he realizes how broken I am.

Which is why it's best to keep away from Dimitri Ivanov.

# CHAPTER THREE

AVA

I HANG up with Gertrude smiling into my empty living room. It's after nine, and I'm home, in my little sleep shorts and a tank top, eating my premade salad I picked up at the market down the street.

She'll cover the position starting the day after tomorrow. She needs a day to get her affairs in order before she can move into Dimitri's home.

I know Dimitri was hoping for tomorrow, but this is a very quick turn around and I hope he's pleased.

Even thinking about him makes me warm all over and I throb again between my legs. I shake my head, wondering if my body has gone into complete revolt over the whole twenty-five-and-celibate thing.

I stand, starting to pace the room as I look down at my phone. I need to call Dimitri, but his voice is going to further amp my overwrought system.

I clear my throat, remind myself to be a big girl, and push his name, having added his number into my phone this afternoon.

It rings several times and goes to voicemail. "Dimitri, this is Ava from Temps For You calling. Sorry for the late hour, but Gertrude has committed to working for the next two weeks as your nanny while we find you a more permanent placement. If you have any questions, call me. This is my cell so feel free to call anytime. Goodnight."

I hang up, blowing out a big huff of air. Done. I didn't even have to speak with him. Though, even his voice message has the blood rushing in my ears. Just hearing that honey baritone…

Phone still in my hand, I pick up the plastic container to toss it in the trash when my phone rings.

I nearly jump out of my skin, the sound jars me so much. I look down, a jolt of energy coursing through me to see his name on the screen.

I quickly toss the container in the recycling bin and pick up the phone. "Hello?" Shit. Why do I sound breathless?

"Ava," my name in his voice makes me stop in the center of the room, my eyes sliding closed.

He was gorgeous in person, but over the phone…

I can just enjoy the sexual sound of his voice while I picture his face and those broad shoulders. No worries about actual touching or how I might freak out.

This flash of fantasy zips through my mind of him holding me in his arms as he stands, my legs wrapped around his waist…

A throb of pleasure so intense it nearly makes me gasp, tightens my muscles. "Hi, Dimitri." God. I sound like I feel. Needy. Wanton. I clear my throat, trying to get myself under control.

"I got your message," he says, his low voice humming through me as I slide down onto my couch. "The day after tomorrow is excellent. Thank you."

"You're welcome." I resist the urge to touch myself. This is a professional call. He's a client.

"And Gertrude is a two-week option?"

"I know for Anna's sake, consistency is better, but Gertrude is a wonderful short-term placement with forty years of experience, who will help train whoever takes over in two weeks."

"I can see why you came so highly recommended." The deep, even tenor of his voice makes my body arch. God. I'm practically humping air.

"That's very kind. Thank you." I clear my throat. "I told Gertrude to report at nine in the morning. She knows that this is a seven-day-a-week placement for the next two weeks. For your more permanent nanny, however, at least one day off a week is required by law. Like I said, if you need seven days a week coverage, two nannies will be necessary."

"I understand. I'll consider everything you've said, and I look forward to meeting the candidates."

He isn't having any trouble remaining professional. He sounds relaxed, at ease. Maybe he just doesn't feel the attraction I do.

Which actually makes it easier for me to get myself under control. This isn't going anywhere and it's all in my head.

"I'll start reviewing files tomorrow, I'll contact each of the candidates, gauge their interest in the position and their suitability as well. Once I've narrowed it down to three or four possibles, we can conduct interviews together at either your home or my office. Your choice."

"Excellent, Ava. I look forward to it."

"Good."

"But also..." His voice gets deeper, richer, and I go completely still. "I look forward to seeing you again as well."

My lips part as I try to mentally calculate what that means. It's personal but not too personal. Like I can't tell him I don't date, but it requires some sort of response. "Thank you?"

He chuckles low and deep. "Until then." And then he hangs up. I pull the phone from my ear, looking down at the screen. I'm going to be giving my vibrator a workout tonight.

In my dreams, my fantasies, I'm not afraid of a man's touch. I don't worry about being hurt. In fact, I do all manner of dirty deeds with men that are tall, dark, handsome and masculine.

And now, I think my dream man is going to change to one who has a touch of gray at the temples.

If only I could get out of my own head and enjoy a man's touch for real.

But it doesn't matter because it will never happen.

Sighing, I open my phone, staring at his name. Even looking at the letters typed in my phone makes me flush. I might just go to bed…

I toss the phone on the couch, flopping back. I cannot use him as fantasy fodder. I have to face him, conduct interviews with him, maintain some semblance of professionalism.

I grab the remote, turning on the television. I ought to keep my focus on Cadence, though Steve's words calmed many of my fears.

She planned this. She's probably gone on some epic adventure. She might need to dry out in rehab after, but this isn't a crisis.

Not finding anything on the television I want to watch, I pull out the files I brought home to review for a long-term nanny for little Anna Ivanov.

I sort several of them into potential candidates or definitely not. Finally, around eleven, I quit and go to bed.

My sleep is restless, filled with dreams about Cadence and then Dimitri.

When my alarm finally goes off at six, I'm relieved to just get up. I pull on my workout clothes and head down to the gym in my building and then return to my apartment for coffee and a yogurt parfait.

Showering and dressing in my favorite dress pants and a cute draped, silky shirt, I collect up my work from the night before and head to the office. The bus ride isn't too long, and I've given up trying to work with the bus stopping and starting so I stare out the window.

I was up early enough that I put rollers in my hair and it hangs down my back in loose waves that I always love.

The bus arrives at my stop, and I slide out of my seat and down the aisle. "Bye, Harry. Have a good day," I call to the driver.

"You're a peach, Ava," he responds with a wink. Harry is in his sixties and nicest guy you'd ever want to meet.

I grin back over my shoulder, but as I look forward again, I stop dead as I run into a solid wall of chest.

I gasp, my hands coming up to meet hard muscle, my eyes snapping up to meet a familiar gaze. Dimitri. His arm wrapping around my back.

That's when my surprise turns to fear, my eyes going wide as the color surely drains from my face. I try to yank back, but his grip is too tight.

I can feel my chest tighten, my breathing becoming erratic as my vision tunnels.

"Ava," he says in that even, calm voice that settles me enough that I don't start thrashing wildly.

"Dimitri," I croak out. "I didn't see you. I thought..." And then I look down to see Anna strapped in a stroller next to us. The sight of her makes me relax as I swallow down my fear, easing back from his large frame.

That's when I realize the bus hasn't pulled away yet. "You all right, Ava?"

"Fine, Harry. Thanks." Now my cheeks are infused with heat as I shake my head at my own stupidity. I've made a fool of myself.

"I did not mean to frighten you. My apologies." Dimitri's hand is still at my waist, and I take another step back so I'm out of his reach.

"It's fine. I just didn't see you. It's my fault. I wasn't looking." I try for a bright smile but I'm out of sorts and I'm sure my lips just look stretched thin.

"Come," he says, holding out a single hand to me. "Sit for just a moment. Recover yourself."

I shake my head. "I should..."

"You should take a few breaths."

I'm shaky enough that I nod. His hand at my back, he pushes the stroller with one tattooed hand, crossing the street and opening the door to a shop.

The smell makes me pause, the sweet scent of pastries delightfully comforting as is the beautiful case of treats displayed before me.

My mouth drops open. "How have I not been in this place?"

Dimitri leads me to a chair, then unstraps Anna. "It's run by a distant cousin of mine on my mother's side and happens to be a favorite of both Anna's and mine."

Anna, let loose from the stroller, makes a beeline for the case, hands and face pressed to the glass that separates her from the pastries.

I lean back in my chair, drawing in a deep breath as Dimitri follows his daughter. An older man comes out of the back and embraces Dimitri, thumping him on the back.

It hits me. When I first saw Dimitri, I thought…that maybe he was following me. It's his intensity.

Or his tattoos. They're seriously aggressive.

But clearly, he was coming here and us running into each other was a coincidence. Have I passed him before? Not even noticed?

That makes me relax as I let out a long slow breath.

"Alex, this is my new friend, Ava. She's helping us find a nanny for Anna."

I start to stand but Dimitri's hand comes to my shoulder, settling me gently back in the chair. But this time I don't panic under the weight of it. It doesn't feel predatory, but protective and if anything, I relax under his touch.

I think it might be the first time in my life that's ever happened and I want to melt into him. "It's nice to meet you, Alex," I say, starting to recover myself from the fear that stole my breath on the street. I find myself reaching up and wrapping my fingers around Dimitri's wrist. I can feel his pulse, strong and constant under my fingers and my cheek bends toward his arm.

"And you, Ava," Alex says, his accent much thicker than Dimitri's. With a wink, he whisks Anna up in his arms and carries her behind the case, allowing her to choose her treat.

Dimitri doesn't sit. Instead, he bends down, keeping his hand on my shoulder, as he whispers close to my ear. "You're all right, *milaya*. Nothing will hurt you here."

I have no idea what the Russian word means but I lay my cheek on his forearm, my eyes sliding closed. "I'm sorry to have bothered you. It's not anything you did, it just happens sometimes."

"What happens?"

But I can't answer as a plate of treats arrives on the table. "I'll get you both a coffee," Alex adds. "Raf. You'll like it, Ava."

"What is it?" I ask, even as Anna toddles up to me, lifting her arms up, a treat in her hand. I pick her up without thinking, settling her on my lap so she can reach the other pastries.

Dimitri's hand slides down my arm and then settles on my waist. It's intimate and comforting and I kind of want to sit in his lap the way Anna is in mine. "It's a sweetened coffee that tastes a bit like espresso."

It sounds delicious.

"Help yourself to a pastry," Dimitri squeezes my waist. "No one can bake like Alex."

I do, taking a chocolate-covered sweet and helping myself to a large bite. I'm a healthy eater. With my curves, I gain weight pretty easily, but I can't resist taking another bite as the flaky chocolate goodness melts in my mouth. It's like the pastry is feeding my soul.

Or maybe that's Dimitri. He chuckles. "I should make you eat about ten of these."

"Why?" I wrinkle my nose, even as he reaches up his other hand and swipes his thumb at the corner of my mouth, removing a tiny bit of chocolate.

I flush at the intimate touch, my chin dipping as I kiss the top of Anna's head to hide my embarrassment.

"Because. You'd look good if you filled out."

Why does it not feel weird that we're discussing this? "Most of the world would not agree."

"Most of the world is stupid."

I smile around another bite even as Alex returns with two coffees and a juice in a straw cup.

I spend enough time with small children that I steady the cup as Anna grabs with two hands, tipping the straw to her lips.

Dimitri's hand slides between me and the chair, settling on the small of my back. "You're a natural with her."

"Experience," I answer with a shrug. "I did a year as a nanny before I was promoted onto full-time staff."

Dimitri, who is still squatting, leans over to kiss Anna's cheek. But it means his jaw slides across my breast, my nipple instantly peaking. My silk shirt is thin enough, it's totally obvious and I'm mortified.

But he only gives me a slight smirk, his eyes full of a mischief that makes me ache as he says, "Try your coffee, milaya."

Automatically, I pick up the mug with one hand and take a sip. But I can hardly attend the flavor, my senses overloaded by the man who is still looking up at me like he knows the most beautiful secret.

# CHAPTER FOUR

Ava

Dimitri and Anna walk me to my building and then we part ways. Though I try to concentrate, I'm working on Anna's nanny applicants for much of the day, which means my thoughts are filled with her daddy.

Like they wouldn't have been anyway.

He's interested, it's obvious, just like it's completely clear that I am too.

But I've been down this road.

The last guy I tried to sleep with, I honestly stopped breathing and passed out right in the middle of everything. I thought I was having a heart attack and the date ended in the ER. He was really cool about it, but never called again, as if I could blame him.

But I like Dimitri so much more than I ever did those other guys I tried to sleep with, and I don't think I could take it when I watch the interest die in his eyes.

So, I try like hell to push him out of my thoughts.

I finally give up on working in the office and head home, bringing my files with me.

Changing into my pajamas, I pull the folders back out. I've got the initial ten candidates. I'm going to review them all again and then start placing calls for screening interviews.

I don't notice when the sun goes down, or how much time has passed until my phone rings, jarring me out of my work stupor.

I nearly jump and then pick up my phone, flushing when I see Dimitri's name on the screen. "Hello?"

"Hello, milaya." That rich baritone slides over me as I sit back on the couch, noting that it's completely dark outside. How late is it?

"Milaya. What does that mean?"

"Sweetheart."

"Oh..." I press a hand to my cheek feeling the heat. "But Dimitri..."

"Don't bother arguing, milaya, I'm very stubborn in this way."

I nip at my lip, placing my head on the back of the couch. "Is that what you were calling to tell me? That you're stubborn?"

"No, I thought I'd see how you were doing."

"The search is going very well—"

"Not the search," he interrupts. "You. How are you?"

"Oh," I whisper into the phone. "I'm fine. Really. I hope I didn't worry you, my job is to make you feel like you're in competent hands not—"

"You are very competent. But I also frightened you. Why?" He sounds curious, but still relaxed. It keeps me from growing tense.

I let out a small sigh. "It's nothing. Thank you for checking on me, but I am honestly fine."

"I'm glad you're fine. Tell me anyway, milaya."

My lips press together as I shake my head. "Honestly Dimitri, I wouldn't even know where to begin. This isn't appropriate and even if it were, this is not a part of myself I share with anyone."

The only person who knows all my secrets is Cadence.

He pauses, the silence filling me with tension, before he lets out this low hum. "No one?"

I shake my head and then realize he isn't in the room. "No. I've never—" I stop myself, sliding down until I'm lying on my couch. "Maybe I should have told someone, but I don't think this is the time or place to start."

"I'm very strong, and fairly worldly. I might understand."

My breath whooshes from my lungs. He is both, I have no doubt. What's more, the words he's asking me to share have been a bit of a festering wound on my heart and head. But once I tell him, he won't be interested in me any longer, past experience has taught me that. "I'm not sure..."

Then again, maybe that's a good thing. Closing my eyes, I already feel tears forming in the corners. "It's not really a worldly story. I was...I was raped when I was seventeen."

He rumbles out a string of curse words in Russian that I don't understand, but I get the point. "Who? A boyfriend? A stranger?"

I suck in a jagged breath, willing myself to remain relaxed. He hasn't hung up yet. But once he knows what a totally fucked up life I've had...

All he's seen is my professional veneer, that's why he's interested in me. "I don't think—"

"Tell me."

For some reason, I can't seem to resist his direct commands. "My mom died when I was eight. Cancer. I was in foster care until I was eighteen."

He makes this noise that sounds almost like a growl.

But the words are tumbling out now. "It was my last placement and at first, I thought it was the best. The couple took in both me and my friend, who is really like a sister. But then the husband..." I can't even bring myself to say his name.

I still have nightmares sometimes.

"Why did you become frightened at my house during the home visit?"

I'm relieved he didn't ask for more details about the attack, but his question throws me. I look at the phone for a second before I bring it back to my ear. "I wasn't—"

"You were, Ava, and I'm curious what I did that frightened you. Tell me."

I draw in a ragged breath. "It was the look in your eyes."

"Hmm." He doesn't sound angry or hurt. Just thoughtful.

Do my words make sense to him? They barely do to me.

Silence stretches out between us and I shift on the couch. "Have I weirded you out?"

"Weirded me out?" he asks, like he doesn't quite understand the words. Or maybe he's realized his mistake.

I let out a long sigh. "Look, Dimitri, I get it. I'm way too much. We can forget this whole conversation, I'll find you a great nanny, and we can just go back to our professional relationship. It's fine." I'm giving him the out. It's enough that he listened. Asked. It's more than anyone has done for me in a long time.

"Milaya," he rumbles, the sound of his voice making me forget all my discomfort as I grow instantly wet. It's deep and possessive and through the phone there is no fear, only raw desire coursing through me. "I want you to put your hand down your pants."

"What?" My heart starts beating double time.

"Touch yourself."

"I don't think—"

"You like me, I know you do, and I like you too. I'd like to touch you, but I think that's going to take some time."

"You're not actually willing to wait for me—" I blink up at my ceiling, trying to understand the right turn this conversation just took.

"I can assure you that I am. Now, I'm going to start by telling you that I think you are the most beautiful woman I've met in a long, long time."

My hand comes to my waist, brushing my tank top up to run my own fingertips over my bare skin. "Really?"

"And if I could touch you, I'd start by kissing you, slowly, deeply, my tongue teasing your mouth open, until you yielded and then our tongues would tangle together."

I draw in a little gasp, the throb deep between my legs pulsing with need. "Are we standing?"

"Do you want to be?"

"Yes," I answer quickly, ready to keep going. More than willing to play this little game. Phone sex had never occurred to me, but now that I'm here, it sounds like the best idea I've ever heard. Like this, I'm free to enjoy his gorgeous voice, the image of him touching me, and it's better than any fantasy I've ever imagined.

"Why?"

My mouth twitches as I frown. "I get frightened when a man is on top of me."

"We're standing," he answers in this rough, masculine voice that brokers no argument and puts me right back in the fantasy.

My hand slides under the elastic waist of my shorts. "Is one of my legs wrapped around your waist?"

"Definitely. One long, shapely leg is around my waist so I'm pushing right against your sensitive clit, making you moan my name."

I do, arching my back as my finger pushes against the sensitive bud. "Dimitri."

"Lifting your shirt, I kiss down your neck and then take one of your nipples in my mouth."

Both of them peak and I give a soft cry, I hold the phone between my shoulder and ear so that I can palm one of them myself. Even with my tank still on, my nipple responds, growing harder, tighter at his words and my touch.

"I'd flick my tongue over the tip…" I hear his clothes rustling and the idea that he's going to touch himself too makes the throb intensify. "Tell me what your nipples look like."

I blink. I love hearing him, but me talking…

Then again, I don't want to stop. Taking a long drag of air, I try. "Umm, they are pink."

"Pale or dark?"

"Pale," I whisper.

"Mmh, yes, milaya, I bet they're gorgeous."

The rosy color of my cheeks is now flushing down my chest.

"How big?" He gives a small grunt. "The size of a quarter?"

"Bigger."

"Yes," he hisses. "Are you touching yourself?"

My fingers sink deeper into my folds. "Yes."

"Good girl," he rumbles, his honey voice, rougher, darker now, in a way that only makes me hotter.

I'm flicking a nipple with one hand, my middle finger flying over my clit, my breath coming out in short little gasps as I breathe into the phone.

"I'd kiss a path down your belly." He's breathing heavy too.

"Are you touching yourself too?" I ask, wishing that I could see him. Touch him. I don't have to be afraid in this moment and with the fear gone, all the desire I've been denying rises up threatening to overwhelm me.

I want to see him. His body, his cock. I bet his big, masculine hand looks insanely good wrapped around it.

"Yes, my sweet treat. I've got my cock in my hand just picturing what you look like with your fingers buried deep in your pussy."

It's dirty enough and so hot, that those words tip me over, and suddenly, I cry out, an orgasm ripping through me. "Dimitri," I cry, my voice raspy as I picture him here, between my legs, his thumb on my clit rather than my own finger.

"Milaya," he pushes out between gritted teeth before he lets out a long groan. My hands clench into balled fists wishing that I could touch him. Slide my palms over his skin.

The line is quiet for a moment, nothing but the sound of our breathing.

As I float down from the orgasm, I feel my body heating again, but this time, it's from embarrassment and not passion. Did I really just do that?

But the memory makes me smile. It's the first time I've shared any kind of sexual experience with another person like this. As embarrassed as I am, it was also really wonderful. "Dimitri?"

"Yes, milaya?"

"Thank you for that. It was…"

"I think so too." I smile at his words, turning on my side.

"Bright side," I laugh a little. "No risk of pregnancy."

He doesn't laugh back and I tense, worried that I made some jump, like he'd even want to have real sex with me. I open my mouth to tell him to forget it, when he answers. "You'd make the most beautiful babies, Ava."

The words I'd been about to say die on my tongue, as I picture myself holding a baby of my own. Suddenly this deep longing fills me that I didn't even know existed. It chokes me with emotion. "I don't know if I could ever..."

"Be kind to yourself and take it one experience at a time."

Does that mean we might do this again? I don't ask, I don't want to put any pressure on him. But all at once, I realize, I am going to have to see him again. "Thank you." But I can hear the hesitation in my own voice and he hears it too.

"What's wrong?"

"I... is this going to make working together weird?" I ask, wincing.

"Not at all," he answers easily, confidence making his tone smooth.

We talk for a few more minutes, until I've relaxed again, stopped worrying that I've made a terrible mistake and then we hang up the phone.

I lay there, half asleep after the amazing orgasm, knowing that I should get up, brush my teeth, and go to bed.

If Dimitri were here, would he pick me up and carry me? The fantasy doesn't frighten me.

He looks so strong, I bet he could do it easily. And in my fantasy, instead of being afraid, I feel so safe and protected in his arms.

My eyes slide closed, I'm so relaxed, I know I'm going to fall asleep right here on the couch.

That's when my phone rings again.

I jolt awake, a smile playing at my lips. It's Dimitri. I know it.

But when I pick up my phone, it isn't Dimitri's name I see on the screen but Steve Imperian's. My investigator.

My brow furrows as I quickly pick up the phone. "Steve?"

"Hey, Ava," he says but he doesn't sound happy. I can already tell something is wrong.

"Did you find something?"

"Yeah," his voice drops low, a wince lacing the single word. "I was able to track Cadence to a last known location."

"What does that mean?"

He lets out a long breath of resignation. "Three days ago, she stepped into a Bratva whorehouse. Well technically, it's a sex club, but that's kind of the same thing. Crazy state we live in."

"What?" I cry weakly. Those words don't even make sense.

"She wasn't struggling. I know that. She walked in of her own free will. But while several people saw her go in, no one saw her come out."

"A whorehouse? But why?" A lead brick sits in my stomach as I sit up. "She wouldn't…"

Did Cadence sell herself? Was she in trouble? Is she still? Is she alive?

"I can't find any record of debt. And no drug dealer she owed, so I can't tell you why. But what I do know is the place is owned by a high-up Bratva captain, his father rumored to be the leader of a major Russian family. If she's still there, I won't be able to touch her, Ava, and neither will the police."

I try to breathe but the air is ragged as it passes my throat to fill my lungs. "No." I shake my head. There has to be some way. This is Cadence. My friend. My sister. My savior. I can't lose her, I have too… "I know someone. A Russian. Maybe he has some information."

"Unless he's connected, I doubt he can help. Dimitri Ivanov is untouchable to anyone who isn't Bratva."

Steve's words are like cold water being dumped over my head. "What did you just say?"

"He'd have to be connected, your friend."

My heart is racing in my chest as I try to organize the chaos of my thoughts into words. "You mentioned Dimitri Ivanov."

"Yeah. That's the guy who has Cadence. Or, at least, he owns the club. Trust me when I say, tangling with him will be the last thing you do, Ava. I'm sorry, but this time, you can't save her."

Tears start tracking down my cheeks. It can't be…

Cadence is my sister.

And Dimitri…it must be someone else. It can't be the man who just made me feel safe.

The man who holds his daughter like she's the most precious thing in the world and plays the piano beautifully.

Then again, he's also the man with creepy tattoos all over his hands.

I shake my head, focusing on Steve. I have no idea how common the name is. Maybe… "Dimitri Ivanov, what do you know about him?"

"Ava. I just said, leave it."

"Tell me anyway."

He lets out a heavy sigh, like's he's not happy with my question. I hear him run a hand through his hair. "I don't know much about him, other than he's connected, and he has a monopoly on the sex trade here in Vegas."

I choke back a sob. Dimitri lives like a king. That penthouse, the artwork…but it can't be the same man. The Dimitri I know is…

"He's around forty, a widow, with a young daughter. Who the fuck knows what happened to the wife."

I let out a squeak, unable to control it because this is all sounding so familiar.

Steve misunderstands. "Sorry. I don't mean to scare you. This guy is bad news."

I don't answer as a soft sob breaks from my lips.

"Sweetheart, where Cadence went, you can't follow."

I look down at the phone. Me and Cadence, we're family. And it turns out, that in fact, if Dimitri really is the man who has her, I actually can.

# CHAPTER FIVE

Dimitri

I look down at the ridges of my six-pack now covered with my own cum. Fuck, I needed that.

I grab a couple of tissues, cleaning myself. I lied to my little milaya when I told her that she was the most beautiful woman I'd seen in a long time.

She's the most beautiful woman I've seen. Ever. Hands down, as the Americans say. No contest.

It's the thick, blonde hair and the big blue eyes, the perfection of her features, the generous lines of her curves.

I love her confidence and the way she squares her shoulders and tackles problems. Smart and sassy, she's this perfect combination of sweet and competent that drives me wild.

But even more than that, I love the way she touched my daughter, the way every line in her body softened when her eyes met Anna's.

I told milaya I was a quick decision-maker, and that is the absolute truth. In that moment, I made a decision. She's going to be mine.

My wife and mother to my daughter.

I'm going to wrap her in a protective bubble so tight, she'll stop being afraid.

Before I was forced into my father's business, I studied the brain and the effects of trauma. I know exactly how to help my little milaya.

There are a few problems, however, I'm going to need to address first. Well, really, there is only one. And it's not her past. That will just take patience and care. I've got both.

But my father. The head of the Ivanov Bratva. He's an issue that cannot be set aside.

I look down at my hands, covered in Bratva tattoos, permanent evidence of where my loyalties are supposed to lie. I received them on the day I was supposed to receive my post graduate degree from Stanford University. They are meant to be a constant reminder of his power over me.

I don't say this lightly…I'd kill him if I could. A sadistic fuck who is a true and diagnosable narcissist, he has no heart or soul, he's tortured his own children for years.

I've spent years rewiring my own mind to undo his cruelty and malice. There is nothing in that man worth saving.

And I'm fairly certain he'd kill me too. I think he's been trying. Stirring trouble in Las Vegas with powerful men who might very well do the job for him. Is that his plan? I'm guessing, yes.

Originally, I was sent here to do his bidding in Las Vegas. Buy the casinos that he uses to wash his money, oversee the drug trade that makes him a hefty profit.

I agreed on one condition. I got to take over the sex trade completely. Reluctantly, my father agreed. If he likes to mistreat his children, with women, he's a filthy animal.

So, I wash his money, run his drugs, and in exchange, in one corner of the world, I keep the women who work for us safe. And a few of them, I can help.

No woman participates in an act she doesn't choose. Activities remain on site so guards can intervene if necessary.

It's not much when it comes to my father, but it's something. Some part I can control.

Like I said, I'd kill him if I could, but I haven't seen him in five years or more, he guards himself against me.

And he lords the safety of my two sisters over me to keep me in check. But that's going to end soon enough. I'm about to make the first major move in my end game, checkmate on my father.

I push up, stretching. What Ava doesn't understand is I need time too. Time to eliminate my father as a threat to her happiness and mine.

Time to save my sisters from his tyranny.

Which means we can have as much phone sex as she likes, slowly build to a physical relationship.

No one knows how badly abuse can affect a woman like I do. My father broke my mother until she was nothing but a shell of a person.

I'll guard my daughter, save my sisters, and I'll fix my little milaya's broken wings. I don't bother putting my shirt back on as I stride into the hall. I hear Anna fussing and I head into her room, reaching down on her toddler bed to rub her back while she sleeps.

She was pulling her ear this afternoon and I'm worried she might have an infection setting in.

I comfort her with soft words in Russian before I rise again, heading to my room. Relaxed as I am, I may as well get some sleep in case Anna is up in the night.

Just as I've stepped into my room, my phone buzzes in my pocket. It's not uncommon for me to receive calls at night, but one of my men wouldn't be calling if it wasn't an emergency.

But as I pull the phone from my pocket, Ava's name appears on the screen.

Answering the call, I'm smiling before I've even brought the phone to my ear. "Miss me already, milaya?"

She gives a nervous laugh, her voice tight with a tension I don't understand, but don't like at all. "Actually," she starts, and I hear her shift, her clothing rustling, "I need to speak with you about the nanny position."

I straighten up, my eyes narrowing. Her voice has taken on that professional tone she used the first day. But under that, I can hear fear. "What's wrong?"

"Nothing's wrong. Well...I hope you're not too upset...."

I wait, tension tugging at my previously relaxed muscles.

"Gertrude isn't able to make it this week after all."

I let out a frustrated grunt. I need to get back to work. I've sold a casino to my Las Vegas rivals and have plans to sell two more in order to arrange a marriage between my oldest sister Katarina, and one of the Smith brothers. Their eldest brother is a duke in England, and my father, power-hungry fuck that he is, has agreed to the match because being part of a royal family is his ultimate goal.

It's how I'm finally going to draw him out.

But what he doesn't know is that I've promised the Smiths two more casinos and a potential second marriage. It would remove my sisters from my father's influence and cut his financial ties to my business, in addition to allowing me to go legitimate. Once he finds out...

Once he finds out, he'll try to take back his business. It will be the opening I need to end this once and for all.

"Don't worry," she keeps talking, her voice breathless in a way I've never heard her sound before. "I'm going to fill in myself while I search for a long-term nanny."

I stop. Ava under my roof? Tucked in my house with my daughter? "You're going to come stay with me, milaya?"

"Well. That's the awkward part. I'll be there professionally and..."

My brows lift. Is she trying to tell me I'll have to behave? I'm a man of iron control and infinite patience.

But I'm also a shameless opportunist. If the potential arises to further my cause, I'll take it. "I promise not to do anything you don't wish for me to do." She'll want everything I give her.

"Good. Because you'll be my employer, and I cannot fraternize even over the phone. It would be highly unprofessional. And our professions are of the utmost importance."

I pull the phone from my ear, looking down at it as I try and puzzle that one out. What does she know of my profession? I bring the phone back to my face. "Indeed."

She gives a nervous laugh. "So, I'll see you tomorrow at eight in the morning?"

I run a hand down my bare chest, my muscles bunching with tension. Having Ava here is a dream come true. But something is wrong. I can hear it in her voice. "Tomorrow at eight."

"All right then, I'll see you tomorrow."

"Ava?"

"Yes?"

"Say my name." It's a simple request, but she hasn't spoken it since we got on the phone and I want to hear it now.

"I don't—"

"Say it," I softly command, already noting, that for all her professional confidence, she bows to my commands.

"Dimitri," she scoffs, irritation or anger lacing her voice. What the actual fuck? Did I push her too fast? She seemed really into the intimacy on our last call.

I breathe out through my nostrils. I'll have to find out more tomorrow. Maybe I'll spend the morning here, going through Anna's routine. "I'll see you tomorrow, milaya."

"Tomorrow." She hangs up then, leaving me to look down at my phone again.

I scrub a hand down my face, frowning, when my phone rings again.

This time, it's Trent, one of my foremen. He came with me from Russia, a former man of my father's. "Yes?"

"Sorry to bother you so late, avtoritet."

"Something wrong?" He wouldn't call if there wasn't.

"Today we had a PI sniffing around the club."

"PI?"

"Private investigator. Asking all sorts of questions about Cadence." He lets out a breath. "Should I tell Zane?"

Cadence is a girl with no family and a very checkered past. Why would an investigator be asking questions about her? "She was clean, right? No drugs and no debts?"

"Not that we could find."

"And we're sure there was no family?" We carefully pick the girls who join The Hunt for this specific reason. We don't want anyone looking for them.

"Sure," he answers. "Her mother died last year from an overdose. She was the last living blood relative."

"Pay the investigator a visit. See if he'll talk. No force this time, offer him a carrot, not the stick. I need to know who is asking the questions."

"Done."

I hang up the phone. I am so close to wrapping up a long-standing problem. I don't need another one knocking at my door. I'm going to have to deal with whoever is causing problems and trying to track down Cadence.

# CHAPTER SIX

AVA

I SWIPE my hands down my leggings, hoping that I made the right clothing choices. Most nannies dress for getting down on the floor and playing with children, but Dimitri's home is not most places. And he is not most men.

A fact of which I've become intimately aware. My stomach turns as I enter the lobby of his building.

The doorman doesn't ask me any questions this time. Instead, without a single word, but with a friendly smile, he moves to the elevator, opening the door.

As I go to step in, he holds out his hand, a key dangling from his fingers. I open mine, palm up, the cool key dropping into my hand as I close my fingers.

"In case you enter the building and I'm attending another resident," he says with a nod. "It only works on this elevator and only you, me, Trent, and Mr. Ivanov have a key."

I'm honestly surprised Dimitri already trusts me with a key. I have no idea who Trent is, but I'm sure I'll meet him soon enough if he's one of the few key-holders.

The tiniest bit of guilt slides through me at the level of faith Dimitri has shown. But I stiffen my spine and nod back to the doorman before stepping into the elevator. I heft my duffle bag higher on my shoulder, determined to look like I belong. I don't really travel, so I've never bothered with nice luggage, but right about now, I wish I'd bought something newer than this old beat-up duffle I carried from one shitty foster home to the next through high school.

I blow out a breath, trying to dispel the nerves that are making my muscles tense.

Seeing Dimitri today feels like so many layers of strange, I don't even know where to start.

I had phone sex with the leader of the Las Vegas Bratva, and then took a position in his house as his nanny so that I can track my lost friend.

Jesus, that's messed up.

Even worse, I'm going to have to control both my attraction and my panic while in his company, all while hiding my real reason for being there.

Easy peasy.

At least Anna is the cutest little thing I've ever seen. That part will actually be easy. And maybe my panic will be a natural wall to place between us.

The elevator slides open as I try to paste a smile on my face.

Dimitri must hear the doors, because he appears a moment later, devastating in a crisp white dress shirt and slacks.

The smile slides right off my face, my jaw falling open as I stare.

"Milaya," he rumbles, Anna appearing at his side, grabbing onto his pant leg.

"Aya," Anna points with a smile.

Despite all the anxiety I had leading up to this moment, Anna mixing my real name and Dimitri's nickname, melts my heart.

I slide to the floor, sitting on the marble as my bag sags next to me. "Anna," I coo back. "I'm so glad to be here with you."

She smiles and then starts for me. "See my dolls?"

I reach out a hand, letting her little hand fold into mine. "I'd love to see your dolls."

I stand again, keeping her hand in mine as she leads me to her room. Looking back, I catch Dimitri picking up my bag and easily slinging it onto his shoulder. I hide the wince to see that beat-up, dirty thing against his Italian wool slacks.

Instead, I focus on the little girl pulling me down the hall. We turn into her room, a large dollhouse sitting in the corner.

Dimitri doesn't follow, taking my bag into my temporary room instead. I can't believe I'm going to live with him. It's insane.

My boss is furious. I'm supposed to place nannies, not become one. I had to promise to forgo my next three vacations and keep up with all my regular work while I did this.

Anna squats down in front of the wooden structure, intricate in every detail.

It's built with center hinges so that it can be opened and closed to reveal the entire inside. It's open now, exposing all the rooms within the house, the furniture, and the dolls. "It's beautiful," I gush, dropping down on my knees next to her, to look inside.

Anna grins, reaching inside. "See this?" She's pointing to the baby room, which looks a great deal like her own.

"Wow." I touch the doll bed coverlet, the material a plush velvet.

She grabs up all the dolls. There is a little girl. A daddy. A grandma. A mother and a little baby boy.

Anna places the daddy in the office. "Daddy goes there."

I hide my smile.

"What are you grinning at?" Dimitri rumbles sliding down next to me.

I stiffen again, and then chide myself to remember to relax. My body cannot give away my every feeling. "At least she didn't set the daddy doll in the bathroom."

He rumbles out a laugh and I find myself relaxing. I know what I know about him. About who he is and what he's done. But I also know that he isn't likely to hurt me here or now. What he'll do if he finds out the real reason I'm here is a worry I'll have to consider later.

"Not right," Anna holds out the mother doll to Dimitri.

"Why not, my little love?" he asks taking the doll and turning her over in his hand.

Anna touches my hair. "Hair is yellow."

Does she want a doll version of me? My brows shoot up and my heart twists. I slide my hand over the dark silky strands of her ponytail. Whatever I do, I have to make certain Anna is not hurt in all of this. She's an innocent in every way.

Dimitri takes the doll in his hand, his thumb sliding down the doll's synthetic hair. "You want a doll with yellow hair?"

"Yes." Anna nods.

Dimitri hands the doll back to Anna, kissing her chubby little cheek. "I'll see what I can do."

He gets up again, leaving the room, but returns a minute later with several sheets of paper in hand.

Sitting next to me, he stretches out on the thick carpet, his long legs looking lean and sexy in his dress slacks.

On my other side, Anna starts to babble about how the baby needs to go to sleep but all I can do is watch Dimitri from the corner of my eye. "This is a list of daily activities for Anna. They are color-coded by ones you need to attend, and ones that are drop off like pre-school. Home visits are in green. I've provided all addresses and contact information, but I have a driver who knows all the locations and travel times for you." He hands me the sheets.

"This is very organized." Apparently illegal activity takes a lot of planning. Makes sense when I think about it.

"Thank you," he chuckles. "I'm going to work from the apartment today so that you can ask any questions you might have throughout your first day."

I scan over the pages, relief making my shoulders sag. There are several spots in each day that Anna is at school or engaged with other services. "Anna has a speech therapist?"

I catch a slight grimace on Dimitri's face. "Between the two languages spoken at home and her mother's…" He looks away. "She's been very slow to speak. But she's catching up now and doing a wonderful job." He gives Anna a soft smile.

"Aya," Anna curls her hand a couple times, calling me forward. "This doll. Baby. Needs bed."

"You want me to put the baby to bed?" I ask, leaning forward. I hear Dimitri's soft growl and turn back to realize that in bending over, my butt is really close to his face. He's staring at the roundness of my ass in leggings, his gaze dark in a way that makes me sit back up, a little zing of tension making me stiff. "How should I put the baby to bed?"

"Sing," Anna giggles. Then she hands me the mother doll. "Rock in the chair."

I set the dolls up, having no choice but to bend again. I don't look back, and Dimitri doesn't make a sound, but I can still feel the tension radiating off him.

Even worse, I respond, growing damp between my thighs. Which means, this time the tension is not fear…

I do as Anna requested, slowly rocking the tiny chair in the dollhouse and sing. Anna joins me humming away.

That's when Dimitri touches the small of my back. It's a light brush of his fingers, and in his relaxed position, stretched out on the floor, it doesn't frighten me at all. In fact, I pulse with need even stronger than I felt before last night.

It's like now that my body's had a taste…

His phone rings, interrupting the moment. He pulls himself up, taking the phone from his pocket. "Hello?"

Immediately, he begins speaking Russian as he leaves the room.

I stay with Anna, playing with various toys until an hour later, when the speech therapist arrives.

As soon as they're settled, I dart to my room and fire off a series of texts to potential candidates for Anna's full-time nanny. I'd like to keep the search moving so Dimitri doesn't suspect why I'm really here.

With that in mind, I slip from my room, making my way deeper down the hall. I know Dimitri's room is here along with his office.

His door his partially open, his deep baritone rumbling into the hall.

"I know what I've told them, and what I haven't. But it's time to be honest. I need the Kincaids and the Smiths if I'm going to take him down."

Take him down?

What does that even mean? It doesn't sound good.

"Make it happen. Tonight, if you can."

Then he hangs up.

I hear the squeak of his chair, and I realize my mistake. I'm about to be caught eavesdropping. I start down the hall, glad for the leggings and sneakers.

But even at a run, I hear his door softly swing wider and I spin back toward him, like I'm just coming out of my room.

"Milaya," he says in that voice that never fails to send sparks shooting through me. "Is Anna with the speech therapist?"

"Yes," I nod with the manic energy of someone who is trying to cover her real intentions. "Is there something I should do while she's receiving services?"

He shakes his head. "The time is yours."

He stops in front of me, his eyes devouring me and my breath catches as I try to decide if the emotion pulsing through me is still fear or if it's just attraction. Both?

He reaches into his pocket and pulls out a card. "The day after tomorrow, Anna has preschool for four hours. I took the liberty of making you an appointment."

And then he hands me the card and I stare at it, trying to understand what's just been handed to me. "An appointment for what?"

"She's a leading therapist who specializes in trauma like yours."

I stare at the card and then at him. "I'm...I...what?"

"If you don't want to attend, I understand. But it's an excellent opportunity to speak with someone about your past. Your fear."

He leans over and places a light kiss on my forehead, before he straightens again. "Anna's favorite snacks are bananas, goldfish crackers, apples, and club crackers."

Then he turns and heads back to his office.

He got me a therapist? This is the man who is holding my friend captive or worse…

I look down at the card. There must be some kind of mistake. Then again, my past has taught me that men are rarely what they seem.

I've got to be so careful with Dimitri Ivanov.

# CHAPTER SEVEN

Dimitri

I look back at Ava who is fingering the card I gave her and biting her lip. She's been withdrawn today, a bit leery of me.

I pushed last night with what we did on the phone. I'm patient, but I'm also an alpha through and through. I will not sit by and let her keep me out with walls.

I have every intention of knocking them down and then rebuilding them to let in the light she's been denying herself.

I step into my office, wishing I could spend the day watching her and Anna together. Every time the three of us are in the same room, I feel this certainty that we're meant to be a family.

I wince to think of Anna's biological mother. I never felt this for her. Despite my business, I rarely have casual sex. It's the indulgence of a weak man.

And it was a moment of weakness, when my father cut all my ties with my sisters to keep me under his control, that I slept with a woman I hardly knew simply for the comfort.

She was one of the madams at my highest yielding club. Everyone knew she was interested, but when my father denied me access to Katerina and Sasha, I'd gone to the club, gotten really drunk, and ended up in bed with Nadia.

I don't even remember the sex.

When she told me she was pregnant, I'd stared at her in complete confusion. A month later, however, the DNA test confirmed the baby in her womb was mine.

I'd married her shortly after. Though I didn't love Nadia, I believe in raising children in the sanctity of marriage. She was the mother of my child, she deserved my protection and the luxuries that I could afford to give her.

Nadia had been thrilled with my proposal, but things between us quickly soured. She could sense my ambivalence, and she grew increasingly resentful that she only had my respect, not my affection.

After Anna was born, she began going out late at night, drinking heavily.

I sigh as I run a hand through my hair.

I will never regret Anna. But meeting Ava, I know how I should have felt during my first marriage.

I turn into my office, softly closing the door.

Pulling out my phone, I dial Trent.

"Boss," he says as he picks up. "Your timing is impeccable."

"Why's that?"

"I'm just leaving the Private Investigator's office." I hear his car door close.

"Get answers?"

"A few," he replies so that I can hear the grimace. "He slipped and used the 'she' pronoun. And whoever she is, he's interested. I can tell by how defensive he got on her behalf. This isn't just a job, he likes her, so getting him to give up her name is going to be challenging."

I frown. Men get very protective when their heart or their cock are involved. Fuck. I could use force, but breaking those sorts of laws can have real and immediate complications. Ones I don't need.

"The Kincaids have all kinds of intel collection devices. I'll call them to see if we can have that meeting tonight. Add this to the agenda."

Trent pauses. "You think they'll help you? After all they think you've done?"

"It's worth a try."

"Instead of involving them," he says sounding tense and leery, "I can call Zane and have him check Cadence's phone. Identify her female callers."

"We will if we have to, but I'd prefer not to interrupt his work unless absolutely necessary."

"Understood." Trent clears his throat, like he's gearing up to say something else.

I straighten as I wait. Trent's been a good number two. We aren't friends, but we share a common goal, making my father pay, and that has kept us bonded together.

"About this plan to speak with the Kincaids. I'm not certain—"

My eyes narrow as I try to understand his opposition. He's never questioned me like this before, and he'd usually be in favor of turning enemies into powerful friends. "What don't you like about it?"

"They're as likely to use the meeting to strike against you as they are to listen."

I let out a long breath of air. I need allies. My father has them in spades. In addition, it was my father who poisoned them against me in the first place. He either wishes for them to kill me, or he just doesn't want me having powerful friends. Either way, I'd be smart to undo my father's work. But I don't explain that to Trent.

The decision is mine to make and the risk is mine to take. "Noted."

I hang up the phone, drawing in a breath. It's not a meeting I'm looking forward to. These men think I've committed a great many atrocities against them. I've allowed it because I wasn't ready to move against my father. Now I am.

Pressing Triston Smith's name in my phone, I listen to the ringing of the line. "Dimitri," he rumbles into the line with his smooth British accent.

I have to give the Smiths credit in one department, their ability to glide through any situation with manners and grace has made them major players.

"Triston," I reply. "How come the wedding plans?"

"Mine? Excellent. My brother Ryker is a bit more anxious about his. When does he get to meet his bride?"

"Actually, I'm hoping to discuss that very topic with you. Any chance you can meet tonight?"

"Just me?"

"No..." This moment has been a long time coming. "I'd like Ryker, Killian, Mason, and Jake there minimally."

"That's a lot of men to get together tonight."

"It's very important information." Once I make this move, there is no going back. I know that.

"How important?"

I blow out a breath. "Life-changing."

Triston pauses. "You better not be shitting me, Dimitri."

"I'm going to pull the skeletons from the closet. It will move all of us forward." That is the complete truth, and he must hear it, because he grunts.

"I'll make it happen, but I choose the location."

"That is fine with me. I'll come alone."

"Alone?" He sounds genuinely surprised.

I get it. It's a dangerous decision for me, but I'm trying to prove myself. Ryker has agreed to marry my sister. It was the first move in making these men allies. It's time to make a few more. "This one is about trust. I come alone."

Silence stretches between us for a moment, then two, before he finally answers. "My house. Ten tonight."

"Good. See you then."

I bury myself in my work for the rest of the afternoon and evening, catching the occasional sound of Anna and Ava in the house. It takes everything in me not to join them.

But finally, as the evening wears on, I step out of my office to find them in the kitchen.

I don't like having a lot of support staff in my space. I have a cleaner that comes in a few times a week and a meal service that delivers food.

I find Anna and Ava at the table together, Anna eating macaroni and cheese, and Ava with a salad.

Ava might have one of the most perfect figures I've ever seen in clothes. But she could stand to gain a few pounds, of that I'm certain.

Opening the fridge, I pull out some sliced pork. "This cut is one of my favorites," I call. "Want to try some?"

"I'm fine, thank you," Ava answers.

"Me," Anna says from her seat. "Please."

With a smile, I cut some smaller pieces, putting them on Anna's plate, and then I take one and hold it toward Ava. "Bite?"

She hesitates and I reach over, gently placing the piece between her lips. I'm hardly touching her, but I still see a wariness in her eyes before she opens her lush lips and lets me place the piece between her teeth.

Her mouth is as gorgeous as the rest of her and my muscles tighten as my fingertips brush her lips.

My plan is to touch her often and without sexual intent. I want her to be comfortable with my hands, my presence. To feel safe in them both.

She closes her lips and chews the pork, her eyes closing. "That is delicious."

"Have more," I answer, returning to the island to cut several more slices. Then, carrying the board over, I scrape them onto her salad.

"Bossy," she rumbles but stabs her fork into the salad, taking a bite of the pork.

I smile, because much of the awkwardness is gone, I touched her without her stiffening, a definite desensitization occurring, and she's eating the kind of protein she really ought to have more often.

"I have a meeting tonight, I won't be back until late. Is there anything you need before that?"

"Not much. Any tips on bedtime?" Ava asks between bites.

"Three songs, lots of hugs and kisses, but only ten minutes," I say then turn and wink. "She'll keep you there all night if you let her."

Ava softly laughs. "I see, and thank you for the information. That's very helpful and very wise."

"You think so."

"My mother never indulged those things with me either. I guess kids need love, but they also need...boundaries."

"Very true." I sit down next to her, my arm lightly brushing hers. "Do you think your mother made a difference for you? Even though she left you so young?" I watch as Ava brushes her fingers over the locket around her neck. I'd wondered where it came from and now I know. It was her mother's.

My own daughter doesn't have a mother. Something I'm hoping to change. I look down at my plate to keep from frightening Ava with another possessive stare.

"I have a best friend. She never had a real mother, no boundaries. I think she's struggled more than me because of it, even though our experiences were very similar in foster care."

Her friend seems like someone who should come see me. But that is not a part of my life Ava should know about yet, so I don't mention it. "I'm sure you're right. My father was too much discipline..." An understatement. "And not nearly enough love."

"Hmmm." Ava gives me a soft smile. "You're not that kind of father at all."

"Thank you," I return, taking a large bite of the food in front of me. I can't dally too long, but as I finish the bite, I lean over and brush a light kiss on Ava's temple.

It's a peck, nothing more. Ava gives me a small smile as I settle back into my seat. There is no wariness this time as she gently nips her bottom lip. She always looks beautiful but sweet and a bit vulnerable, pulling on every male instinct I possess. I want to pull her in my lap and kiss her senseless.

I don't. That isn't what she needs just yet.

A comfortable silence falls before Anna holds out a piece of macaroni and cheese to me between pudgy fingers. "For you, Daddy."

I do not like macaroni and cheese but can't resist my daughter, and

I take the piece from her hand, Ava's eyes laughing, as I make an exaggerated, "Mmm. Delicious."

Anna smiles and then gets another piece to feed Ava. I'm well aware I started this, and I'm so glad I did as I watch Ava eat the piece of macaroni from Anna's hand.

This is the exact kind of moment I pictured. And I know that Ava belongs here with us. No one is getting in the way of that.

That's a promise. And I keep my promises.

# CHAPTER EIGHT

Ava

Dimitri leaves shortly after dinner and Anna and I spend the evening together.

We read books, play with toys, but toward bedtime, she gets very quiet. I assume she's tired until she melts into my lap and I feel her head. "You're warm, sweetie pie."

"Cold," she answers, snuggling deeper into my body as she tugs on her ear. "It hurts."

I wince, lifting her in my arms. Heading into the hall bathroom, I find a swipe thermometer and brush it over her forehead. Numbers flash and finally pop up on the screen. Shoot. She's got a fever. "Over a hundred," I murmur.

Picking up my phone I realize it's almost nine. Pressing a few buttons, I dial Dimitri and wait as the line rings.

He picks up on the second ring. "Milaya?"

"Hey. Sorry to bother you."

"You are never bothering me. What do you need?"

I feel heat slide through me at his words. Even my relationship with Cadence doesn't feel like this. If I'm being honest, things have been weird with Cadence lately, even before she disappeared.

Longer stretches of not talking, her hinting she needed a change, telling me that I needed to start getting out, start really living life.

I sigh. "It's Anna. She's got a fever, and she says her ear hurts."

"Damn. I knew it. Give her the Children's Tylenol in the medicine cabinet. I'll call the emergency line and make an appointment for the morning."

"How much?" I ask, seeing the bottle on the shelf next to where I found the thermometer.

He gives me the dosage and I nod along as Anna buries her face in my shoulder, giving a soft little groan. "Oh, sweetie pie," I coo. "You'll feel better soon. Promise."

Dimitri is quiet on the other side of the line. "Go ahead and give her the dose. I'll wait."

"I know you have to work," I say as I take the bottle down, removing the dosing cap.

"It's fine, Ava, you'll know all of this soon enough, and besides, I like hearing your voice."

I give the bottle a one-handed shake and then remove the cap while still holding Anna. I almost correct Dimitri that I'm only here for a few weeks, but I purse my lips instead as I pour out the medicine.

I know why I'm here, what I want to accomplish. But is it wrong that part of me is really enjoying being in Dimitri's house, next to his strength?

It's like exhaling after holding my breath for a long time. I almost tell him that I love his voice on the other end of the line too.

That it makes me warm, but I hold my tongue as I bring the little cup to Anna's lips. She drinks down the medicine and then curls back into me.

I coo, rubbing her back as I snuggle her to my chest, giving a soft bounce of comfort. Dropping my cheek to the top of her head, I start for her bedroom.

Dimitri makes this back of the throat rumble. "I wish I was there with both of you."

The words are so…intimate. I let them wash over me. I wish he was here too. I am in so much trouble. "Does the fever change bedtime?"

"Most likely, yes. Especially with the earache. It helps to keep her upright."

"All right," I nod along with Dimitri's words.

"I'll be home as soon as I can."

"Home," I repeat, looking around. This place, for all its grandeur still feels way more like a home than my place ever did.

Maybe it's the way I can feel Dimitri's strength in the furniture, or the fact that he clearly loves his daughter so much. Or how the kitchen is stocked with healthy and delicious meals.

I hug Anna tighter.

"Are you all right, sweetheart?" he asks into the line.

How can this be the man Steve talked about? He's full of contradictions that just don't make sense. "I'll be fine. I'll see you soon?"

"Soon," he murmurs.

I hang up, hating to let him go.

Taking Anna into her room, I get her settled into her pajamas, grab a blanket and return to the living room, where I snuggle us into a recliner.

With her body molded to mine, I wrap her in the blanket, rubbing her back.

She's restless at first, shifting as she tries to get comfortable.

After a bit of fussing, she falls asleep. Kissing her head, my own eyes get heavy. We're warm and cozy, her weight on my chest a comfort. It's been the craziest day.

I haven't learned much about Cadence, but it's only one of the many mysteries I can't tease out.

What I really need to do is learn more about the man I live with. He holds all the answers I need. Not just about Cadence.

Or even what kind of man he is.

I'm beginning to realize, I have a lot to learn about myself too.

# CHAPTER NINE

DIMITRI

I PULL up to the giant gate outside Triston's house. It's so risky to be here alone. Not only will there be several men here who consider me their enemy, but I've come to Triston's home where he could have set up any number of traps for me to fall into.

These men believe that I bombed one of their clubs, shot up Killian Smith's apartment.

I blow out a breath. My first job will be to tell them the truth. Then the negotiations can begin.

The gates swing open, my driver rolling the car through opening and driving up the long drive to the mansion that sits set well back from the road. A wall encases the entire property, all of it meticulously landscaped.

The Smiths own an empire, and this is their crown jewel.

At least here in the States. Their eldest brother has the vast English real estate that goes along with the title of duke.

My driver stops, and I open my door, climbing out of the car.

Making my way up the stairs, a uniformed woman opens the door, showing me, not up the stairs, but toward the back of the house.

We move into a well-appointed kitchen where several Smith and Kincaid men gather around an island.

"Mister Ivanov is here," she calls to the assembled group.

"Thank you, Mrs. Raith," Triston answers stepping away from the group and toward me, reaching out a hand to shake mine before he gestures for me to join the others.

I do, and looking down at the counter, note a large tray of nachos in the center of the island. Gris Smith, Triston's twin, grabs a stack of cheese and chips, taking a giant bite of one and then washes it down with a beer.

If this more casual environment was meant to relax me, it's working.

I've been to a few executions, and I've never once seen nachos served.

"Glad to have you here," Gris says after he swallows, "We're still waiting on my brother-in-law, Mason."

"Probably tucking in Charlotte," Killian says as he helps himself to a large chip loaded with guacamole. "I didn't think he could get crazier about that woman, but it turns out now that she's pregnant, his obsession has notched up another level."

Triston gives me a side glance, which likely means he doesn't trust me and is worried that information will be used against Mason. "Wait until the baby comes," I answer, matching the casual attitude of my companions. "He's going to reach new levels of protective."

Everyone stares at me. "Is that why you bombed the Kincaids' club? Protection for your child?" Jake Kincaid asks, holding a nacho in midair as he waits for my response.

Jake is older than the others, an uncle to Mason, Leo, and Roman Kincaid. Like me, he's got a bit of gray at the temples, though he married a younger woman who is even more connected to the Vegas underworld than he is.

I breathe in deeply and blow the air out my nose. I'd hoped to wait for Mason before I launched into this part of the conversation. "That's the first bullet point on my agenda. Because the truth is, I was responsible for neither that bombing of your nightclub, nor the shooting at Killian's apartment."

Silence meets my words, disbelief staring back at me from every set of eyes. Killian cracks his tattooed knuckles. "You're telling me that you had nothing to do with those attacks? When you took responsibility already? Makes it hard to believe you."

I twist my neck, cracking one of the vertebrae. Killian isn't wrong. Stepping up to the counter, I reach onto the tray and grab a loaded chip, popping it into my mouth.

Nachos aren't really my thing, but it's good.

I chew, buying time, making them wait, before I answer. "Most of you know I am one hand in a much larger operation." I grab a beer and crack it open.

Behind me I hear footsteps. I turn to see Mason Kincaid enter. He is not the largest, or most muscled man around this island, but every line in his body speaks of power.

I take a slow sip of the beer. "Mason."

"Dimitri." He stops at my side. "You don't give yourself enough credit. I know you're far more than just a hand."

The business I've been able to cut my father out of, the kink clubs, run with efficiency and safety. I don't claim to be a pinnacle of morality, but I keep the people in my employ safe.

My father has very different practices. "I came to Vegas ten years ago to purchase the first casino, the one I sold to the Smiths. The money I used to buy that place, however, was not my own but my father's."

I look around the circle. "In exchange, I bought out his share of the whorehouses, turned them into legal clubs, and cut out the human trafficking because…" It's completely fucking filthy.

"The problem is that many, within my own organization, like my methods better than my father's, and I have been rising in the ranks, getting increasing supporters both personally and financially. With that money, I've been expanding, and I've become a threat."

"To your father?" Mason asks, his brows up as he stares at me.

I grimace. I don't even know how to describe my father. There is no love there, except for himself. What he feels for us is only about power and malice. "I tried to make three of the four casinos legitimate. I've bought two of them myself. But the more I act on my own, the more control I take..."

"The more he interferes," Triston says, his wince not of disbelief but of resignation.

I nod.

"Triston?" Killian asks and Mason stares across the island at the head of the Smith family.

"I've always wondered at the dichotomy in your businesses. There is a kindness in the way you run the sex clubs. You protect the women, it's quiet, controlled. They are valued."

"Shit." Mason mutters next to me and the tension leaves my shoulders. They understand. "He bombed my club, not you."

"He's sabotaging my success so that he can control me. Without allies, I am far weaker."

"And the casino you sold me in exchange for the marriage between Katarina and Ryker?" Triston asks.

"It was his. And he agreed because he wants the connection to your family. But I implied I'd wash his money in the other three establishments, and I don't intend to follow through with my promise. Once he learns the truth, our cold war will get red hot." I don't say the last part. That I'd remove my father from this earth if I could. All he does is sow pain and suffering wherever he goes.

He destroyed my mother, he is attempting to do the same to my sisters.

Triston draws in a deep breath. "We understand bad fathers. Trust me on that." Gris and Killian both nod. "But if all you say is true, how much danger will there be when your sister is a member of our family and you cut him from the business?"

"A lot."

"Forgive me, but I'm not sure I'm ready to believe all that Dimitri has said," Jake Kincaid cuts in. "Has anyone else remembered that he was meeting with the Italians? He tried to make a deal behind our back even when he'd agreed to tie his business with ours."

I grimace. "I was meeting with the Italians. I won't lie to you. But I was neither going to sell them one of the casinos, nor was I breaching any part of our contract." I blow out a breath. "I was hiring them to do a job that I can't."

"What job is that?" Mason asks quietly.

This information does not strengthen my position as an honorable man. "He has my sisters in a prison. He's a threat to my daughter and the woman..." I stop before I say Ava's name.

"The nanny?" Killian asks. Fucking Killian. He can move through shadows like no man I've ever met, and he knows all sorts of secrets, including my feelings about Ava.

"You want to take out your father?" Gris asks, popping a giant nacho in his mouth. "Bold. And fucked up."

"He killed my mother. Slowly. Painfully." I stop, gritting my teeth to keep the rest of my feelings in, though they've leaked out with what I did say.

I shouldn't have said that. While I knew I'd have to offer up some skeletons, I'm too raw on the topic of my mother to use the information as a point of negotiation. And this is about gaining their partnership again, not providing them more fuel to hate me.

But those words seem to shift the mood and not against me. "We know about that too," Mason rumbles. "If I learned anything from my father, it was how not to conduct a marriage or raise children."

We all come to this shadowed life with deep scars. But my daughter and Ava will live in the light. I take another slow pull on my beer. It's not my normal drink, but it creates the proper pauses I need. "I want safety for my family. Security. I'd pay a great deal for that privilege."

"How much?" Mason asks.

"What does safety mean?" Triston follows up. Both are excellent questions. I look across the island at Killian, the shadow, as he pops a chip into his mouth and then takes a drink from his glass of water. He's the one man without a beer.

When he swallows, he gives a near imperceptible nod. "He wants me to kill his father, for one."

"No," Triston cuts his hand through the air. "That is not on the table."

Killian doesn't look at his brother, he stares at me. "I've seen you with the nanny. You love her."

I swallow, not saying a word.

"I didn't start following you until six months ago, didn't begin scoping out your clubs until last month. But I hear the girls that work for you talk…"

I still. "And?"

"They say that you're a saint in sinner's clothing. That they've never been safer. They say they'll follow you wherever you go because they aren't exploited, they are protected. What did he do to your mother?"

I won't tell them all of it. "She was a prostitute. I'm not ashamed, she had more heart in her pinky finger than he does in his whole body. But he treated her like…" I stop, my jaw going rock hard. I can't share her secrets, not in front of strangers.

Killian's hand flexes. "I'll do it, even if you don't close the deal with my brothers."

The air rushes from my lungs as gratitude makes my shoulders sag in relief. I can't get close enough to touch my father. I'm too known. But Killian...

My eyes close as relief washes through me. "Thank you."

"What are the rest of the terms?"

"I want one casino that connects to your tunnel. That will be enough to sustain me. In exchange, I'll sell you the other two at a bargain price." What I want is a legitimate source of income that can provide for my family. A casino on the tunnel will do just that. "And I might need a few phone taps. I can't do them, but I know you can." I look at Jake who still appears skeptical as he looks back at me. But my attention is diverted again.

"And the arranged marriage?" Ryker asks. He's been silent this whole time, his gaze watchful as he listens. It's a smart move to remain quiet. He's learning about me, while giving nothing away about himself.

I should make a point to get to know him. He's the man who is positioned to be my brother-in-law.

"Stands." I say, holding the counter, and giving him a nod of acknowledgment. "But as you meet my family, be warned, my father should not be underestimated and if we fail, my sisters need to be safe."

I still don't know how I'll protect Sasha, but Katarina will be safe married to Ryker Smith.

The pieces are beginning to fall into place.

"Do you have any idea how Killian is going to gain access to your father?"

"He'll come as soon as he learns about the sale of the casinos. And when he does, we had all better be ready."

# CHAPTER TEN

Ava

I PARTIALLY WAKE to the sound of a bell dinging. My eyes flutter as I try to remember where I am and what that noise might be.

But it doesn't happen again, I'm warm and comfy and I immediately drift back to sleep.

I have no idea how much time passes, but at the feel of arms sliding under me, I wake with a start, my eyes flying open.

Dimitri's face is right next to mine, his dark eyes assessing me.

"What are you doing?" I gasp, stiffening away from him.

He tips forward, his lips brushing mine. "Hush, milaya," he whispers. "It's just me, you're safe."

The sound of his voice relaxes me, which is when he pulls me into his chest and lifts me out of the chair.

I should be afraid, but somehow, Anna being sandwiched between us, makes me feel completely secure as he straightens up, taking me with him. "Where are you taking me?"

"To bed."

"But…" My brow scrunches. "She needs to be upright. You said…"

"I did. And I appreciate what you're doing for her, but you need your sleep too. You're already doing two jobs. You don't need to be a parent too."

I sink deeper into his embrace. "I didn't actually mind. Sleeping with her is better than having a weighted blanket."

"Careful," he rumbles, giving me a light squeeze.

"Careful with what?"

"Keep talking like that and you're going to end up with the job full time."

I smile. "I already have a job."

"I didn't mean the nanny position." He starts down the hall, entering Anna's room first.

My brow scrunches. "What are you talking about then?"

He sets us both down on Anna's bed and then rolls her to my side so she's laying on the mattress.

Before I can ask him what he means, he's got me in his arms again.

To my shock, I'm still not afraid. My arms slip around his neck. Is it because this isn't sexual?

Whatever it is, I'm far more comfortable than I've ever imagined I'd be in a man's arms. It makes me wonder why I haven't allowed a man access like this sooner. I tried to go slower… But then I'd stop myself. Maybe I should push a few of my very stringent boundaries. But this isn't the man. In fact, Dimitri is the last man with whom I should test any intimacy. I know far too much about him to pretend he's anything close to safe. "You should put me down."

"You're right. I should. You're going to ruin me," his eyes are dark and stormy and for the first time tonight, I'm afraid of him again. I stiffen, trying to slide out of his grasp but he only holds me tighter.

"Dimitri," I plead. Ruin him? What does that mean? Has he learned the truth somehow? Does he know why I'm here? Panic rises in my chest, and deep down, I feel it.

It's not just that I'm afraid he'll hurt me. It's that he might know I haven't been honest. What will he think of me then?

It hits me right in the gut that I care about his opinion of me, his feelings. And what I'm doing…it could ruin everything.

Am I the bad guy here? That thought makes my eyes go wide and I shake the thought away.

But the fact I care so much already has me letting out a long breath of air.

I can't believe how much he means to me already.

"Because when you hold my daughter like that, it makes me think.... You should be mine."

My mouth falls open. This can't be happening. "Dimitri." He shouldn't like me. I'm here to discover his secrets. And I shouldn't care about him. He's the man who took my friend.

"Sorry, milaya, I'm not putting pressure on you, but I'm also not great at remaining silent when there are words I want to say."

Now that isn't a surprise at all. We pass by my room and keep walking down the hall. "Where are we going?"

This time, I speak with real fear. Because I'm not ready for—

"Hush, I know your fears. I would never push you to a place where I frighten you."

I stare at him in complete confusion as he maneuvers the knob to open the door and then steps into the room with me still in his arms. "Being in your bedroom makes me afraid."

"Give me a second," he answers as he sets me down on my feet next to the bed.

Should I run? Wait? He opens out a drawer and pulls out a set of handcuffs. Who keeps handcuffs next to the bed?

Why is he taking them out now?

I stumble back, but he only tosses the metal rings on the mattress before he starts pulling his dress shirt from his slacks.

Then he undoes the buttons and shrugs off the shirt, pulling the T-shirt underneath over his head.

The muscles of his back ripple, his shoulders so broad, I stop my retreat to just stare. God, he's beautiful.

He kicks off his shoes and then lays down on the bed.

All fear is gone, replaced with intense curiosity as he threads the cuffs through one of the slats in the headboard. "The key is in the drawer."

And then he opens one cuff and closes it around his wrist. "Come, Ava, and put my other hand in the open ring."

"But why?" I stare at him in confusion even as my body begins to heat. Because with his hands cuffed…all I feel is pulsing need.

"I am yours to do with whatever you wish." And then he manages to get his second hand in the cuff. "I can't grab you. You'll have complete control. Do you want to touch my body? Explore?"

The ache starts between my legs, throbbing with need as I move toward the edge of the bed. I just got done thinking he was the last man I should be getting closer to.

"Do you want to sit on my face, have me lap at your pussy until you cum all over me?"

I gasp, a flood of excitement soaking my panties in an instant. "Do you want me inside you? I can't stop you, can't touch you any way you don't want. I am yours to command."

"Dimitri," I plead, his name just falling from my lips. I keep saying it, but it means something different every time I do. This time… "This is a bad idea."

"I disagree. I think it's an excellent idea. I think this will help you experience sexual satisfaction with another person with safety and control."

My mouth opens but then closes again. He's not wrong. "Take off your shirt," he commands.

I reach for the hem and then pause, looking up at the ceiling. "I thought I was in control."

He smiles at me then, settling deeper into the bed.

I reach out a hand, trailing it over his chest. His skin is coarser than mine. Darker. As my finger trails over his nipple, it peaks just like mine would.

I gasp even as he sucks in a breath.

A tent is forming in his dress slacks, and I keep running my hand down his body, over the ridges of his six-pack abs to the narrow belt on his pants. He's so gorgeous and in this moment, he's all mine. I want to touch him everywhere, feel every part of him.

My tongue darts out to lick my own lips as I flick open the buckle and then reach down the with the other hand, using both, to undo his pants.

The tent grows bigger. "Ava."

My gaze darts up to his. "What?"

"What are you doing?"

"You said I could explore. I'm exploring." And then I pull down the zipper. "Lift," I softly command.

The voice that told me I should not do this is barely a whisper, my curiosity and desire drowning it out.

He lifts up his hips, his stomach rippling as I tug the pants and briefs underneath down to his thighs.

His cock stands at attention, large and thick.

I thought it might scare me, but I don't feel fear at all. Only more raw desire as I reach out my finger and trail it over the tip.

A pearl of liquid forms at the opening and, wrapping my fingers around the girth, I brush my thumb over it, spreading it over his skin.

His jaw locks as he leaks more precum. That's when I lean down and flick out my tongue, taking a small taste.

"Milaya," he rumbles out, the sound ripping from his throat. But, for once, I barely attend his voice. I'm transfixed.

This is like some deep fantasy come to life. No fear. No worry. Just exploration, desire, and fulfillment. It's everything I've ever wanted and didn't know how to make happen.

I let go and finally do as he commands, ripping off my shirt and then reaching behind me to unclasp my bra, tossing it to the side.

His eyes drink me in, the desire in them undeniable and tonight, like this, it makes me even hotter. Knowing that he can't grab me, force me, leaves me free to understand that his eyes are just telling me how much he wants me, not that he'll hurt me.

I hook my thumbs in the waist of my leggings and then I shove them down my thighs, knees, and finally off my feet.

Standing back up, I watch him, watching me, the heat of his gaze making me flush.

"Jesus, you're beautiful," Dimitri grunts. "Even better than I imagined."

I don't say anything. I'm not using him exactly, but I'm deep in my own head, finally able to explore all the pent-up need I've buried for so long. "I want to know what it feels like to have you inside me."

"I'm yours, sweetheart. Have your way with me."

I don't wait for more permission as I climb onto the bed, straddling him. He naturally presses against my opening.

There is no pain, no fear, I thought maybe there would be, but there isn't. "Women like this right? They enjoy having a man..." I pause taking a breath before I say the words, "fuck them."

"We are going to make love, milaya, where you feel good, cherished, protected by my body."

My mouth falls open as I look down at him. My hands are braced on his chest, my arms pushing my boobs together as he starts to press inside me.

It feels so amazing, I gasp, arching my back and neck, which only makes him sink deeper.

"I didn't know," I whisper, as I slide the rest of the way down him until he's fully seated inside me. "God, I didn't know. Holy shit, I..."

"Slide back up and then take me in again," he grunts out between his teeth.

This time I don't correct his bossiness, doing as he commands. It feels even better than the first time and I let out a high-pitched, breathy moan to feel the head of his cock moving inside me.

"Fast. Slow. Hard. Soft. Figure out what you like..."

But I'm already rising back up to sink back down, picking up speed with every thrust until I'm bouncing on him like it's an Olympic sport. He feels so good and I never imagined that I'd actually be here, with a man inside me, while the orgasm builds to such heights that I all I can do is chase the feeling, desperate for release.

My fingertips bite into his chest, my head falling so far back, my long blonde hair brushes his thighs.

"Ava," he growls out. "When I get close you have to—"

But I can't listen, my body breaking, the orgasm ripping through me like nothing I've ever felt before.

I scream, frantic as I keep the pace, wanting every last drop of pleasure he can give.

A snarling groan pulls from his lips, and he thrusts up, jerking as his own release fills me with his cum.

That's when I gasp. "Shit."

"Too late," he grits between his teeth, pushing deeper inside me.

My eyes go wide as I stare down at him. What have I done?

# CHAPTER ELEVEN

DIMITRI

AVA STARES down at me with wide eyes, whatever haze she'd been experiencing cleared.

I'm not even certain she remembered my name while she was fucking me.

And that was fucking.

I'm not upset, in fact, I firmly believe she needed that. Needed to turn off the emotion, all emotion, so that she could also quiet the fear and just feel the pleasure.

"Sweetheart," I whisper, soft. Low. Warm. "Lay down on my chest."

She does, curling into me, my cock still nestled inside of her while her cheek presses to my collar, her head fitting in the hollow between my shoulder and neck. "Dimitri?" she says, and I can hear the tears.

I wish I could wrap my arms around her, but they are chained above my head. "I'm here."

"That was…" her voice catches.

"I know." I rub her forehead with my chin.

"I forgot to stop before you came."

"I know."

"What if…" Now there is only a question, no tears.

"You tell me, milaya, if that happens, and then we make some decisions together." She nods into my neck, her body so relaxed on mine, that I smile into her hair.

The long, blonde mane is trailing across my bed, which I appreciate both because the sight of her hair like that does something to me as a man, but also because it gives me a fantastic view of her back. I can see the gorgeous curve of it, the swell of her ass as she straddles me.

My cock inside her starts to swell again.

She stirs, lifting her head. It brings her cleavage into my line of sight. She's got fantastic full tits that have been hiding in her bras and looser silk shirts.

Paired with her flat, toned belly and the swell of her hips, I could stare at her for hours. Paint her. Not that I'm a painter.

I am a pianist. The one advantage to growing up with my father is that we had enough money for lessons and as he wants to be something beyond the thug that he is, he encouraged my passion for music.

He liked that I was good. But I don't want to think about him now.

Her lips are parted, and I remember the sight of her tongue darting out from between them to taste my cum. I swell even larger inside her.

"That feels good," she whispers, her neck arching again. But this time, her belly is pressed to mine.

"That feels good, Dimitri," I correct. I don't care that she used me once. I encouraged it. But even handcuffed to the bed, if she wants to fuck again, she's going to fuck me as she looks me in the eye.

Handcuffed or not, this time, we're doing this my way.

She presses her pelvis into mine, moaning as I hit her clit with my pubic bone.

"Say it, milaya."

"That feels so good, Dimitri." And then her eyes open enough that I can see the haze of passion in them.

"Kiss me," I command as she starts to slide off my cock.

She does as I say, her mouth dropping to mine. I'm aware it's an odd time for a first kiss, I've already cum inside her. But I want to know her mouth, want to add intimacy to the passion.

But as her lips drop to mine, hers soft and so fucking sweet, I lick along her bottom lip to taste more of her.

She moans into my mouth as she sinks down on my cock again. And then her hands slide into my hair as she grips the strands, kissing me deeper. She's grinding against me, her body spiraling toward another orgasm with record speed and I'm right behind her.

This is sex that I will never forget as I deepen the kiss, my tongue tangling with hers. She doesn't retreat from either my tongue or my cock. If anything, she gets more frantic, chasing her pleasure as her tongue licks at me.

I break away long enough to growl out, "That's it. Take the pleasure my body was made to give you."

"Dimitri," she cries against my lips. "I'm going to cum. Oh God, I'm going to—" And then she cries, breaking apart again.

I punch up, one, two, three more times before I cum too, filling her again.

There is every chance Ava could become pregnant. One, we're doing this again very soon, and after feeling her like this, I'm cumming inside her every time.

She wilts back on my chest and once again, I'm still inside her, but this time, she lays on my chest and falls instantly asleep.

I smile, kissing her temple.

My eyes slide closed too. I can't fall asleep yet, I've got to take these handcuffs off. I'm about to wake her when a cry sounds in the monitor.

I'm not surprised. Anna wasn't likely to sleep long if it's an ear infection.

But Ava bolts awake, half sitting up before she falls back down on my chest. "Anna," she gasps. And then she starts to climb off my body.

"Ava. Stop." Anna's cries get louder. "Get the key from the drawer."

She does as I ask, her body on glorious display as she stretches to reach the drawer. She fumbles around, finally pulling the key out of the interior.

Her eyes are unfocused and her movements heavy. "Take a breath."

She does, her eyes clearing a bit. Then she slowly inserts the key into the little lock. I feel the metal give, unlocking from my right wrist.

Pulling my hand free, I grab the key, unlocking the other wrist myself.

Ava watches me, her body still pressed to mine. Out of the cuffs, I wrap my arms around her, rolling us to the side.

There is no fear now, her body completely pliant as I pull out of her and then kiss her mouth. "Go back to sleep. I'm going to get Anna."

"I should..."

"You should sleep."

"Go to my room."

I chuckle. No chance. When I get Anna back down, I'm spending a few hours curled around the woman who is going to be my wife. Even if she doesn't know it yet. "We'll worry about that later. Sleep now. You must be exhausted."

She snuggles down in the covers, her eyes sliding closed. "You're sure?"

"I'm sure." In fact, I've never been more sure of anything in my life.

# CHAPTER TWELVE

Ava

I wake feeling more relaxed and comfortable than I've ever felt in my life. I wiggle my toes and then go to stretch, meeting a hard wall of flesh. That's when I realize the reason I'm so comfortable is because I'm snuggled into the body of another person.

Dimitri's arm is around my torso, his hand on my naked belly, his fingers splayed out to cover my skin. I gasp, trying to sit up.

"Milaya," he rumbles behind me. "Anna kept me up most of the night. Can you at least ease out of my bed instead of thrashing around."

"I'm sorry," I cry, flipping around to look in his face. Which is when I realize my mistake. I'm naked. And he's mostly so. My skin slides over his in the most seductive way as my breasts crush to his chest.

His arm around me, is now perched just above my ass and he slides the hand down to cup one cheek, pulling our hips together.

I have a second to feel frightened before hot lust skitters down my spine, settling between my legs.

But he must have felt my slight stiffening though, because he rolls onto his back, pulling me on top of him.

His nose nuzzles into my neck. "Better?"

"How did you know?"

"I can feel your fear. I don't like it. I only want to make you feel better." He kisses a trail along my collarbone, his other arm wrapping around my back.

My eyes flutter closed. How is this possible? How is the one man I'm supposed to hate, fear even, be the man who is patient, kind, understanding? Who is willing to take the time to help me overcome my own hangups?

It's crazy, but for another moment, I just enjoy the feel of his lips, his muscles moving under my softer body. A sigh escapes my mouth as tingles flutter over my skin.

"That's the noise I like to hear," he rumbles against my chest, his hands gliding up my back.

I think I could have sex like this. His hands on my body, his lips moving over my skin.

I arch my head back giving him more access. Dimitri's touch frightens me less and less, his hands bringing comfort, joy, not worry or anxiety.

I slide my fingers into his hair, holding his head in my hands as I kiss his forehead. "Dimitri."

"Say my name like that again and I'm not letting you out of this bed."

I still for a moment. He makes me feel so wanted. Men have wanted me on first blush, but they didn't stick around when my real self was revealed. Not like Dimitri. "Don't tempt me," I whisper back, my eyes fluttering closed.

"Are you tempted? Because if you are—" The sound of Anna crying through the monitor interrupts whatever he was about to say.

My eyes fly open. "Poor thing."

He lets out a long breath. "I'm sorry to have to cut this short."

"Don't be," I say automatically as I slide off him. I can't resent Anna. Not only is she the cutest little girl, but maybe being a father makes him ideal for me. Patient. Kind. Willing to fit himself around my needs just like he's doing for Anna now.

He gets up, nothing but his boxer briefs hugging his hips and thighs, showing off every delicious, rippling muscle.

My mouth goes dry as I pull the blankets up my body. He looks like a marble statue of a god.

He turns back to me, even as he tugs a pair of athletic pants up his legs. "Don't cover up. Let me see you one more time."

A flush climbs up my cheeks but the ache between my thighs throbs too and I find myself slowly lowering the blankets.

I'm on my side but my shoulders are flat on the mattress, the swell of my hip on full display.

I watch his eyes darken, but this time, it doesn't frighten me, in fact, my breath hitches as his gaze slides down my body. "Do you know how gorgeous you are?"

I must be bright red as I turn away, biting my lip. "Stop."

He slides back on the bed, but he doesn't cover me, which I appreciate. Instead, he kisses my hip bone, looking up at me with an intensity that steals my breath. "I can't. I want you too much."

I'm so hot, my breath is coming out in short gasps. I want him too. I want him so much.

He licks at my skin, one of his hands sliding over my knee.

The idea of him shifting his mouth to kiss me where I'm aching makes this pulse of need move through me.

I reach down, wrapping my fingers around the back of his neck as my legs open in invitation.

I feel him smile against my hip as Anna gives another cry. "The downside of sleeping with a man who has a child."

Is that what we're doing? Sleeping together? "I'd fire me if I weren't the boss."

And if my boss knew, I'd be out on my ass. "We can't have that."

There is so much more I want to say about the future, my fears, as he pushes off the bed, pulling on a t-shirt before he heads out the bedroom door. But I have no idea what would happen if I did tell him the truth.

I pull myself from the bed as well, putting my shirt and leggings back on before I pad to my own room and into the bathroom, where I turn on the shower. The guest bathroom here is more than twice the size as my bathroom at home.

I've been saving every penny, but maybe it's time for me to upgrade my apartment. I basically live for work and Cadence and since coming here, I'm feeling like my life before this has been a bit hollow.

I love Cadence so much.

But there has been some distance between us, and I've been working harder than ever to remain close to her. I will always love her, but maybe I was choking her with how much I need her.

I've been holding on so tight, even before she left. We've always gone through periods where we fall apart more than stay together.

She'd disappear on some adventure, or I'd bail her out of some situation that made her resentful instead of happy.

But there's been this new layer lately. She always seemed to hate that I had it all together. But the last several times we talked, she said she was worried about me. *I didn't have a full enough life...I needed people beyond her.*

I'd dismissed her words. She was enough for me. I didn't want more people, more risk. I turn on the shower, stripping off my clothes.

Turns out, she was right.

Being here has brought color to my life in ways that I never dreamed. I step into the hot spray, the massaging head spraying a targeted stream of water onto my stiff muscles.

I tip my head back, wetting my hair and working the shampoo through the thick strands. I can't think of Dimitri as my savior. It's just going to mean I end up hurt in the end.

And Cadence. I've got to find her, bring her home safe, and tell her the truth. As much as I save her, she saves me too, forces me to see certain truths about myself.

It's always been this way and, it turns out, her leaving was what I needed too. It's so crazy.

An hour later, Dimitri leaves with Anna to take her to the pediatrician. I offer to go, but I'm relieved when he gently refuses. "Catch up on your other job while you've got the time."

But as they leave, and I find myself alone in the apartment, I don't return to my computer.

Instead, I stand outside the door of Dimitri's office, staring at the closed door. Am I really going to do this? Rifle through the private spaces of his home?

I square my shoulders. This is what I came for.

How else am I going to help my friend?

Drawing in a deep breath, I push open the door. The room is exactly how I pictured it, a large mahogany desk sits to one end, a bank of windows behind it, displaying a stunning view of the Las Vegas skyline.

File drawers are built into one wall, framed in more dark wood.

Walking across the floor, I do a quick scan for any cameras. I haven't seen any evidence of them anywhere in the apartment, but I take a second look before I move behind the desk, opening the center drawer.

There is nothing but pens and other office supplies.

The next one holds tape and a stapler, neatly arranged. And the third holds nothing more interesting than more office supplies.

Moving to the cabinets, I open a drawer to find tax documents and payroll for the various casinos. All of it screams legitimate business owner.

Hands on my hips, I let out a breath. It makes sense that Dimitri doesn't leave information about criminal activity out for anyone to find.

But still. I'd hoped for some small nugget. A tiny clue of what he does and where I start my search for Cadence.

Or maybe I didn't. Relief makes my breath come out in a long steady stream.

Searching the last drawer, I leave the office. Crossing the hall, I enter Dimitri's bedroom. I'm more comfortable here, having spent the night last night.

Part of me wants to give up. I didn't find anything, and that might mean there has been some mistake. He's not the man I think he is, and I'm free to just explore what's been happening between us.

But I shouldn't give up now. And besides, if Dimitri were to return home and find me in here, I'd have an excuse that I left something behind last night.

There is no risk continuing my search in here.

I rifle through the nightstand, my only find is the handcuffs we used last night. I touch them, my body getting hot all over, before I move to the dresser. Finally, I search the closet but find nothing more than his scent that wraps around me like a blanket and a reminder that I'm likely a shitty person.

Done searching, I know I need to come up with a new plan. But in the meantime, I might as well get some real work done before Anna comes back and I'm once again taking care of a sick toddler.

The stranger part is how much I'm looking forward to both Dimitri and Anna coming back. Even the short time they've been gone, I miss them.

I care about them both way too much already and If I'm not careful, I'm going to get caught in my own trap.

# CHAPTER THIRTEEN

DIMITRI

I CARRY ANNA INSIDE, tossing her antibiotics on the counter. I've been antsy to come back here, see Ava, touch her skin.

Not that she can't cuff me to the headboard again. It's a small price to pay to be inside her, feel the slide of her body against mine.

I'm not a man who compromises very often. But I want Ava enough that I'm not certain there is a length that is too far for me to go to make her mine.

I break open the bottle of medicine, unwrapping the dropper to dispense the liquid when the object of my obsession appears.

In leggings and a fitted athletic top, her hair piled on top of her head, I like Ava as much like this as I do in her little pencil skirts and silk blouses.

Anna leans out, holding her arms out to Ava, and she sweeps my little girl into her embrace.

Has Anna been missing having a mama? My baby curls into my woman, Ava's chin coming to the top of Anna's head. "Your ear still hurt, sweetheart?"

I fill up the medicine dropper and hold it toward Anna's mouth. "My little printcessa will feel better soon enough."

Anna drinks it down and then curls back into Ava, tucking her hands between their bodies.

Ava kisses Anna's head as she coos. I can't help it. I hook Ava's waist, curling both of them into my body.

Ava doesn't stiffen, if anything, she melts into me, even with Anna's body between us. I wrap my other around them, holding them tightly as my chin comes to the top of Ava's head, the three of us locked together.

We stay like this for a minute or two before Ava finally steps back. "You must need to get to work."

I do. I've missed several calls, including one from Trent, but what's happening in my kitchen feels more significant than anything happening at work. "Soon."

She gives me a small smile, even as she looks away, her gaze fixing on the far wall, a clear sign she's pulling away from me again. My time with Ava is like a spring. We compress, we retract.

That's all right. I'm a persistent man.

She clears her throat. "When was Anna's last dose of Tylenol?"

"Two hours ago."

Nodding, she turns toward the living room. I take a step after her, my hand coming to her hip as I stop her from leaving.

She looks back over her shoulder at me, looking so beautiful and fragile, and the smallest bit frightened. I drop my hand as my chest tightens. She needs my love and support so much, but she's too afraid to take it. "If you need anything, you come get me. I'll be in my office."

She gives a little nod, her lips pursing before she heads for Anna's room. I draw in a deep breath, then two, as I try to calm my surging desire to toss them both in my car and take them far away.

That isn't the way out for any of us. I've always known that, which is why I've held tight all this time. But with Ava here, she's added a new layer to my need to protect. But that's not the move.

Now is the time I'm going to have to fight for our future.

With that in mind, I stride down the hall, past Anna's room and toward my office as I pull out my phone, dialing Trent.

I turn the knob on the door, but it was clearly not closed tightly and I stop, my brow furrowing. I always close the door.

The cleaning crew isn't here until tomorrow.

"Hey, boss," Trent says into the phone.

Leaving thoughts of the door alone, I push it open and enter the office. "Hey. I saw you called."

"Yeah. Did you have the meeting last night after all?" He sounds pissed that I went against his advice. Which in turn pisses me off.

These decisions are mine to make and the consequences will be mine as well. "I did."

"And..."

"It went well." My voice gets harder with every word. This isn't like Trent to question my judgment, and I do not appreciate the change.

"I'd guessed as much since contracts made it to the lawyers, which is excellent news. But..." He makes a clicking sound through his teeth. "You also received an email from your father this morning."

Shit. No wonder he sounds strange. "Did he say what about?"

"He says he's coming here to meet your sister's fiancé, but the timing is awfully suspicious." He clears his throat.

"Yes. It is." I slide into my chair, scrubbing a hand down my face. "We should be ready for anything."

He doesn't answer and I let out a long breath, understanding his silence. "We're going to get your wife back, Trent. My sisters too."

He rumbles out his frustration. "I know. We just have a few too many problems currently. Any word on who is trying to find Cadence?"

"Not yet." I grimace. If my father is going to start making noise, the last thing we need is someone going to the police. If the details of The Hunt were revealed, my entire operation would be in jeopardy.

And I'd end up in prison.

That is one place from which I cannot fight my father. "Still want to wait for Jake Kincaid to pull phone records?"

"No. Call Zane. Have him check Cadence's phone. We need to start eliminating problems."

"Will do."

I hang up, gently setting my phone on the desk. Whoever is sniffing around my business will have to be dealt with quickly. Hell is about to descend on Vegas.

# CHAPTER FOURTEEN

Ava

By the time I put Anna to bed, she is clearly feeling better. I sigh with relief when she falls asleep, and I slip out of her room.

Dimitri left in the afternoon, heading to one of the casinos, and I heard him come home a half hour ago, but he didn't come into Anna's room, leaving me to take care of bedtime, which is a relief.

My goal is to creep into my room without seeing him and then pretend to be asleep.

I'm feeling weird about playing investigator even though that is why I came here in the first place.

Every time I look at him, what I see is the man who is helping me, caring for me, in ways no one ever has before. And I'm repaying the favor by doing my absolute best to betray him.

I've never been good at being the bad girl and I'm struggling hard against my own nature.

I just open my door, about to step into my room, when he rumbles out from down the hall, "Milaya."

"Shh," I respond. "I just got Anna to sleep."

He walks toward me, eating the ground between us. "In that case, come to my room."

"Dimitri," I whisper, worrying my lip. "I shouldn't."

"You should," he says, leaning down to place a kiss on my neck. My skin tingles at the touch and I can already feel myself giving in, wanting him more than I want to hold the line.

But I can't do this. I can't share his bed while I work to expose his crimes and find my friend.

Maybe I could ask him...

This would all be so stupid if he isn't even the man I'm looking for. And I hate keeping secrets. But if he is the man who has Cadence, would he tell me the truth?

Goose pimples break out all over my skin. "Dimitri," I say on a gasp. "This is a conflict of interest. I told you yesterday—"

"I disagree," he rumbles into my skin. "Having you in my house and in my bed feels like the best alignment of interests possible."

"Whose?"

"Mine," he wraps an arm around my waist, pulling me close, my body fitting so perfectly into his. "Now, if you don't want to shower with me, I have another idea..."

My mouth goes dry as my nipples pucker. His last idea was the best night of my entire life. "Does it involve handcuffs?"

He smiles into my skin. "No. But it does involve me crouching down between your legs while I lick you until you scream my name."

I get so wet, I can smell my own arousal and I'm sure he can too. "Oh God," I whisper, one of my hands snaking around his neck.

"Is that a yes?" he licks and kisses his way up my neck toward my ear.

This is so wrong and so right all in the same moment and I draw in a trembling breath, as I shake my head, trying to gain some control over my wayward body. "No. No. I've got to get some work done." It's a feeble, shitty excuse, and my words are flat with my lack of conviction.

Still, he eases back, his brows drawn together. "Did I frighten you, milaya? I'm sorry if I did." His hand cups my cheek. "I'll slow down."

I don't want him to think he's scaring me when I feel braver than I've ever felt before. "It's fine. I just..."

"It's all right," he soothes, his other hand running lightly down my arm, making goose pimples break out all over again. "I can be as patient as you need."

Crap. He's making this so much harder.

Feeling like a complete jerk, I nod and then dart into my room, closing the door. Leaning against the solid wood, I draw in a ragged breath.

I don't want to fight him. I want to let him keep healing me.

Pushing off the door, I cross the room and pick up my phone. I'd stopped trying to call Cadence when I took this position, but I hit her name, listening to the line ring. I need to hear her voice, remember why I'm here.

The call goes to voicemail. I listen to her message, tears forming in the corners of my eyes. "Leave a message if you're brave enough."

I shake my head at her words, always stirring up trouble. I miss her so much and I'm worried.

When the tone sounds, I squeeze my eyes shut. "Hey, Cade, it's me. I just wanted to hear your voice and also tell you...I know there were times I should have fought harder for you. But I'm fighting now. It's tough for me, I know you know that. But for you, I'd go to the ends of the earth. I'd fight all the way. I love you."

I hang up, my hand pressing to my mouth as I fight back the tears. They're no help at all, and they'll only drain me of the energy I'll need.

That's when my phone rings. I look down and my eyes nearly pop out of my head. It's Cadence!

"Cadence?" I cry into the phone.

"No." A deep male voice rumbles back. "Stop calling, Ava. Cadence doesn't want to speak to you."

And then the line goes dead.

I let out a strangled cry, my hand coming to my mouth again to cover the sound. A broken sob breaks through my hands as I sink to the floor.

Whatever I feared just came to life in one man's gravelly voice. Cadence is in trouble. "Now I lay me down to sleep…" I whisper into the room. This time I need to do more than just lay on the bed, like I did when Al came at her. This time I'll fight.

# CHAPTER FIFTEEN

Ava

Despite trying, I barely sleep and am dragging myself out of bed the next morning. Even when I was asleep, my dreams were filled with nightmares, my past and Cadence's melding together to leave me feeling raw and exposed.

I wish I'd been in Dimitri's bed with his body wrapped around mine, his strength making me feel safe. I know it would have staved off the nightmares.

Would he be able to help me with Cadence if I asked?

I'm competent, hard-working. But I'm out of my depth with what's happening with my best friend, and I don't know how to move forward.

Standing up to a man like the one I heard on the phone...

Blood rushes in my ears. It's my worst nightmare. I draw in several jagged breaths, trying to calm my racing nerves.

Dragging myself into the shower, I stand under the hot water, trying to relax. I'm both wired and exhausted.

I finally leave the bathroom, getting dressed, and, drawing in several deep breaths, I open my door and step into the hall.

I am hit by the smell of coffee and bacon, a combination that instantly perks me up.

Heading out into the kitchen, I find Anna already in her booster chair, scrambled eggs in front of her.

Without a word, Dimitri hands me a cup of coffee. "Thank you," I sigh, taking the steaming cup from his hands. "I need this."

"Rough night?"

"Yeah."

"Up late working?"

"No," I wince, remembering I told him I had work to do. I wish that had been the case.

"Worried about today?"

"What's today?" I ask, my furrowed brow meeting his over the top of my mug.

"Your appointment with the therapist I made for you. Remember?"

I lower my mug, my eyes going wide. "Appointment?" He'd told me, but with all that's been happening, I completely forgot. Which is so not like me. "But what about Anna?"

"Normally she'd go to preschool. But with a fever yesterday, I thought it best she stays home. So...I called in the speech therapist for an extra session."

Dimitri went through so much trouble for this. But the idea of digging into my past, today of all days... "I don't..."

"It will be good for you, milaya."

"But I've been doing so much better with you," I softly answer, taking another swig of my coffee.

"You have." He smiles over his shoulder from his spot at the stove, before he comes around the island, dropping a light kiss on my forehead. "But I really think that a therapist will help you come to terms with your past."

"Dimitri," I softly plead. God, I want to hide in this man's strength, let him wrap me up and protect me from the world.

I bet a woman who has a man like Dimitri never has to worry about other men hurting her. That thought makes me hold the air in my lungs as my eyes go wide.

His hand comes to my jaw, softly cupping my face. "I can reschedule if you'd like. But I want to help you, sweetheart. Know that."

I know he does. That's the crazy part. It hits me again. That Steve thinks this is the man responsible for Cadence's disappearance. "No. You don't need to reschedule. I just forgot. I…I'm not myself."

He puts his arm around me, pulling me close. A week ago, I couldn't imagine being touched like this. Now, I sink into him, burying my face into his shirt. I draw in his scent like it will infuse me with his strength.

"Ava," he whispers close to my ear. "I'm worried about you."

I shake my head against his shirt. "I'm fine."

"Are you sure? Am I… I'm pushing too fast, aren't I? You seem far less balanced than when we first met…"

"No." I lift my head then. This embrace, it's holding me together when I might have fallen apart. "I…I'm having trouble with a friend. I…" I want to tell him. All of it. Let it pour out of me.

His hand slides behind my neck, supporting the weight of my head. "Oh, milaya, I'm sorry. Let me know if there is anything I can do to help."

My mouth opens as words threaten to fall out. I want to tell him everything. Even what Steve said. I want Dimitri to tell me it's not true. And that he's here for me, that he'll help me with Cadence. "Thank you," I whisper as his lips brush lightly over mine.

"I'm here for you, Ava."

My heart swells in my chest as I clutch his forearm with one hand, the other sliding around his waist. "If you could give me the address to the therapist…"

"I'll drive you," he answers. "It will be easier."

Then he eases back, gesturing to my coffee. "Drink up. And have some breakfast. It will help."

I do as he commands, feeling slightly better for eating.

Fifteen minutes later we're out the door, taking the elevator down, not to the lobby, but a floor lower, to the garage.

Right next to the doors, in a private stall, is Dimitri's car. It's black and sleek, though I don't even know how to drive so I have no idea what kind of car it might be.

"Go ahead, it's unlocked." He gestures toward the passenger door.

I'm about to tell him that he's brave to leave his car open in this city when I look around and realize, the garage is for him alone and a metal door closes in the space. We climb into the car as the metal gate clangs open and Dimitri backs out the car.

The seat hugs me, the interior smelling of rich leather. "Your car is beautiful."

"Thank you." He looks over at me and winks. "Want to drive? It's not just a luxury sedan, it's got excellent horsepower."

I'm not even sure what that means. "I don't know how," I whisper.

I see his brows lift as he steers into traffic. "You don't know how to drive?"

"Foster care in the city," I shrug. "Most of the families I lived with took in kids like me for the money. They didn't have cars, and if they did, they didn't let me drive them."

His mouth presses into a line. "I'll have to teach you."

My mouth opens and closes. There he goes again, righting every wrong in my life.

The drive to the therapist's office is short, the building beautiful. We park and he takes me up to the fifth floor where we enter a sophisticated lobby with plush carpets and comfortable couches.

Sitting together on a love seat, I feel the butterflies rising in my stomach. Despite the comforting interior, I feel out of my depth. I don't talk about my past—ever.

I barely wanted to tell Dimitri and he's the closest I've been to anyone since Cadence.

I slip my hand into his, feeling the emotion welling up in my chest again. I wish I'd slept more or that I wasn't so worried about Cadence.

I already feel raw and I'm going in to talk about my feelings. My worst experiences.

By the time the therapist opens the door, I'm shaking a bit, Dimitri looking at me with a great deal of concern. "You don't have to do this if you're not ready."

I nod, but I still stand. Maybe it will be good. Maybe I won't have to talk about anything other than my complicated relationship with Cadence and how worried I am.

I get up on shaking legs and follow an attractive professional woman into her office.

"Hi there, I'm Dr. Morgan, but most of my patients just call me Hope."

"Hope. That's a nice name for someone in your line of work," I say and she laughs, though I'm sure she's heard the joke before.

She gestures for me to take a seat, and I do, letting out a slow breath of air. "I know that Mr. Ivanov made this appointment for you. Said you could use an ear."

"Maybe," I answer, my breath hitching. "I'm not sure…"

She holds up a hand. "We work at your pace. It's fine if for today, we just get to know each other."

My shoulders go limp. "That's good. I was really nervous. I mean, I'm sure I need to be here. I grew up in foster care and some of the stuff that happened—" I stop, realizing I'm already going into it. Is there part of me that really wants to get this out? My past has been a poison, festering my whole life.

"Anything you want to talk about?"

I shake my head. "I had one friend that I made after my mom died, and we were in a lot of homes together. But lately she's been pulling away, more and more."

Hope frowns. "Sometimes change means shedding the past."

I shake my head, knowing she's right. "She's my family."

"Tell me about her."

I do. I tell her about how Cadence stood up for me and how I'd cover for her when she got in trouble and before I know it, I'm building toward that day that everything changed for me.

This wasn't the plan, I barely know Hope, but I think the memory has been festering and Dimitri has brought my feelings even closer to the surface. The poison is bursting to get out.

Which is likely why the words are tumbling out. "I took a shower after school. When I got out, I wrapped my hair in a towel." I know it seems like a nothing detail, but it explains where I was at mentally. "And then I put on this full-length robe that belonged to my foster mom. She told me to wear it in the hall, so I was covered."

I draw in a shaky gulp of air, my heart beginning to race in my chest. "I opened the door and started down the hall when, from out of nowhere, my foster father jumped me."

My throat burns as much as my eyes. The walls that keep these secrets are especially weak lately and I feel myself going places I never wanted to visit again. "I thought he'd mistaken me for his wife. You know? The towel on my head, the robe. I said, *Hank, it's me. It's Ava,* even as he yanked open the robe and tugged down his pants."

My chest is heaving, and tears have started streaming down my face. I can't keep them in anymore. "He smacked me and told me to shut up and then—"

The room spins and I can't catch my breath.

"Put your head between your knees," Hope softly commands as she comes to my side.

I do as I'm instructed, but as I tip forward the room is spinning terribly, and I fall onto the floor with a thump.

"Ava," Hope cries. "Are you all right?"

That's when the door bursts open, Dimitri appearing in my line of vision. Before I can say a word, he's sweeping me into his arms, cradling me against his body.

"Hush," he whispers against my ear, crushing me to his chest.

I press into him, my wet cheek sinking into the hollow of his neck. "I said too much too soon. I'm just too raw…"

"I know, my love. But I'm here, and you're safe with me."

I snake a hand around his neck. "Promise?"

"No man will ever hurt you again. Promise." He squeezes me tighter as I breathe in his scent.

My heart stops racing, my breathing growing even again as I keep my eyes closed. I hear them discussing me. Another appointment…a safety check, but I can't keep the words in my head.

Only one thought fills my mind.

When did Dimitri Ivanov start feeling like home, and what am I going to do?

# CHAPTER SIXTEEN

Ava

We return back to Dimitri's apartment, him leaving for work, me spending the day with Anna. During Anna's nap time and additional services, I try to squeeze in her nanny search and keep up with work emails and requests.

But in terms of finding Anna a nanny, or any of my work, my heart isn't that into it. I like it here, if I'm being totally honest.

And with each passing day, I'm growing more certain that Dimitri is the man I should ask for help in my search for Cadence, not the man I should be investigating.

By the time I put Anna to bed, I sit on the couch, tired but far more stable than I was this morning.

Whatever I said to the therapist, it's been the equivalent of throwing up. Like I've expelled the poison and now my body can finally recover.

I'm left drained but more balanced.

And I've had some time to consider the man who picked up Cadence's phone. For all I know, that was Cadence's latest boyfriend.

Unlike me, she has no trouble hopping into bed with men. Maybe she didn't tell him about me, or maybe she did.

Maybe she was like, *my former best friend is turning into a stalker.* Which, when I think about it, might actually be true.

I just can't let go of the fact that she might be in trouble. Then again, there is at least some evidence that she chose the trouble. Leaving work like that.

Maybe I've had the whole thing wrong...

I hear the ding of the elevator, and I close my laptop, turning to watch Dimitri walk into the room. "You're home."

"I'm home," he rumbles, moving toward me.

He barely breaks stride as he reaches down and lifts me into his arms, before he settles on the couch with me in his lap.

Things have been so muddled, I've hardly had time to appreciate his strength, or the lengths he's gone to make me feel good.

But I do now, pressing my chest to his as I lean in and kiss his mouth. He feels so good, tastes amazing as my fingers thread into his hair.

He kisses me back, long and slow, before he leans away, looking into my eyes. "I was a little worried you'd be upset with me."

I stare back, my eyes wide with surprise. He's never insecure. "Why?"

"I made that appointment, you clearly weren't ready for it."

I sigh with a shake of my head as I lean back into him. "I feel better for it, and I'm not sure I was ever going to push myself to go." And that is another point Cadence had been trying to make. I need to push myself out of this very tight comfort zone if I'm going to recover, not just exist. I'm starting to really see it.

He kisses me, his mouth guiding mine in a melding that is so filled with simmering passion that it steals the air from my lungs.

I barely notice when he's lifting me again, standing with me in his arms. I've threaded both my arms around his neck, my hands in his hair, my mouth completely open to his.

I don't pay attention to where we're going until Dimitri starts easing down so that my feet are on the floor.

We're in his room, my toes sinking into the thick carpet. I've barely gotten my balance when he pulls me flush against his body, pressing us together from hip to chest, without a bit of air in between.

I moan into his mouth, so ready to be wrapped up in him that I'm irritated by the clothes that separate us.

As if he senses my wish, he fists my tank top in his hands and then starts working it up my body. I step back just enough so he can pull the cotton shirt over my head and then I tug at the buttons of his dress shirt.

But I only make it halfway down the row of buttons before he hooks a hand around one of my ass cheeks and pulls my hips back into the cradle of his.

His rock-hard cock pushes right where I need it, and I have to pause in my pursuit of undressing him to tip my head back and arch against him to feel the full length of him against my body.

With his other hand, he unhooks my bra as I finally get the last button undone. I start shoving the shirt off his shoulder, forgetting that it's tightly cuffed at the wrists.

Which means, the fabric bunches at his hands and doesn't come off. "Shit," I mumble. "Apparently I suck at undressing a guy."

He chuckles, shrugging the shirt back on, and undoing the cuffs so that he can pull the garment off and shuck it to the side. "Your clothes are far easier to remove than mine." Then he pulls the t-shirt he's wearing up and over his head, revealing his bare chest.

I can't help myself, I lift both hands, running them over his muscles, his skin, covered by his chest hair, warm and tempting.

"Take off your pants, milaya," he rumbles, his nipples pebbling under my touch.

I take my hands from him, eager to do as he's commanded. I've lost that hesitation I had before, that little fear that was my first instinct before I remembered it would be pleasure with him.

I yank down my leggings and underwear, even as he rips his belt off, tossing it to the floor.

I'm naked already, his eyes sliding down my body as he kicks off his shoes. "Bend over the bed," he rumbles.

I turn around, doing as he commands. I do feel a small shiver of apprehension then. I'm so exposed...

A soft thud sounds behind me and I look back to see Dimitri on his knees. I instantly relax. I don't know how he does it, feeling my fear, but he does. And every time he corrects, making me feel so safe and secure.

I relax again, my thighs falling apart as his hands run up the back of my legs. "I can smell you."

I can smell it too. We've barely started and I'm dripping wet. I wet my lips, wincing with embarrassment. "I think I'm so new at this, I can't control my reaction—"

"I love the way you smell," he growls and then he leans forward enough to run his tongue up my seam. It feels so good, I gasp in a breath that ends on a moan. His mouth vibrates against my exposed flesh. "I love the way you taste even more."

He called me his love today. I heard it. I'm trying not to read into it too much, but I know that my feelings are getting involved, because I replayed the timber of his voice at least a hundred times in my head throughout the day.

He licks me again, circling my clit with his tongue, making my thighs shake with a desire so intense, it overwhelms me. My fingers dig into the covers, clenching them into fists in the blankets as I bury my face to muffle another moan.

My back is arched so deep, I think I might break, but I'm chasing his touch, the pleasure so intense I can't keep quiet as I toss my head back.

Which means, he only works me harder, hitting me right where I need it. My eyes are squeezed tight, my body trembling so fiercely, I'm whimpering with high-pitched cries. Every time he touches me, it's the best experience of my life.

I'm so taut, my entire body is engaged. "Dimitri," I beg. "I...I..." I let out a keening scream, falling over the edge, an orgasm ripping through me.

He's up before the tremors have stopped, ripping open his pants, and shucking them down to his knees. "I want to be inside you, love."

I look back over my shoulder. That's the second time today he's called me love. Does he know what it does to me? How it makes me feel? "I want that too," I say, our eyes locked together.

Granted, I'm lying and he's on his knees, but looking into his eyes, I don't feel anything but excitement.

He lines his body up to mine, pushing the tip of his cock inside me. "All right?"

"Good." As ever, he's being so careful with me. I'm so appreciative, I actually feel tears misting my eyes. I never dreamed a man could be this combination of strong and kind.

"Are you sure?" he pulls back out and leans over my back to kiss my temple. "You're crying, milaya."

I blink back the tears. "No. Not crying. Or maybe yes, but they're happy tears, promise. I'm just…thank you."

His brows lift, but he doesn't ask as he sinks back inside me, this time going deeper, not stopping until he's filled me in the most satisfying way. We both groan.

That's when he answers, "Don't thank me for doing my duty as a man. Intimacy is built on trust. It's not a gift that a man asks your permission to touch you and only does so in ways that make you both feel good. It's your right."

My breath catches as I stare at him. Everything Dimitri has done and said since I met him has painted a picture for me.

This is not a man who hurts women. Not ever.

This is a man who can be trusted. I feel it deep in my bones. I don't know why I didn't see it before, but I do now. Whatever my doubts and suspicions are, there must be a reasonable explanation for Cadence's disappearance.

He pulls out and sinks back in until he bottoms out. I push up my backside, wanting as much of him as I can get.

He grabs my hips, using the leverage to set the pace until I'm panting with the pleasure that's building inside me again.

How does he make me feel this good? I can't ask out loud, all I can do is clutch the bedding as the ride gets faster.

We're both so close, our lovemaking is starting to lose the art, the steadiness of the stroke, when he reaches around and presses two fingers to my clit.

I explode again, groaning his name as I shatter. He roars, his body shuddering as he cums. I look over my shoulder again, watching the pleasure that pulls every muscle taut. He's gorgeous like this, masculine and feral but also so powerful.

I want to drink him in. Tattoo him in my memory.

His eyes slowly open, meeting mine. My lips part, words I don't dare say crowding my mouth.

I want to tell him that I think I might be falling in love. I want to confide in him about Cadence.

His hand slides up my spine, moving between my shoulder blades before he wraps his hand around the back of my neck. "You must be tired."

I barely slept last night, and two amazing orgasms have completely sapped any energy I have left.

My eyes flutter closed. "I am."

He gives a small laugh. "No falling asleep yet. Let me get you under the covers."

"I can go back to my room," I answer, making no attempt to actually move.

His arms slide under me, turning me over as he lifts. I wrap mine around his neck, kissing behind his ear as he pulls down the covers and settles me on the mattress, covering my body back up. I snuggle in. "Are you coming to bed with me?"

"You know I am," he answers, moving around the bed. "Last night was ridiculous, you in your room and me in this large bed all alone."

That makes me smile, a small laugh breaking from my lips. It was ridiculous. I turn on my side as he climbs and wraps his larger body around mine. He feels like heaven and I sink into the embrace, already half asleep as I hum out my pleasure.

That's when his phone rings.

I jerk awake, my brow furrowing even as he rolls away. "I'm sorry, Ava, I have to take this."

"Of course." But he's already sitting on the side of the bed.

He answers the call still naked. "Trent?"

I remember the name, know that this is one of his most trusted men.

I hear the low rumble of a male voice, Dimitri's body stiffening with every word.

His head whips around, his eyes narrowed at me, the accusation in his gaze stealing my breath. "I'm going to need you to repeat those words," he rumbles sitting taller. "How does Ava know Cadence?"

I gasp in a breath, sitting up, as my whole body stiffens. This is bad. Very bad.

# CHAPTER SEVENTEEN

Dimitri

"Ava Tantor was in foster care with Cadence," Trent repeats. My free hand clenches into a fist, the potential betrayal of these words slicing at my stomach.

There is no way that Ava is here by coincidence. Which means, she's come under false pretenses.

This is the woman I've fallen in love with. The one I want to be the mother of my child. The one I've treated with nothing but respect and kindness.

And she is connected to the last female player of The Hunt.

"She is the person who has been calling Cadence over and over."

"No."

"Yes," Trent answers with a rumble. "Thanks to Jake Kincaid, who has apparently installed cameras across from your house, we have actual video footage of her searching your office while you were taking Anna to the pediatrician."

"He told you this?"

"Emailed you, actually." I close my eyes. Trent checks my email daily to clear any emails I don't need to take time answering, so it makes sense he'd see the email first. "I've deleted the email, so you don't need to see it. But I pulled records from Cadence's phone, then traced Ava to the temp agency, and finally to your house."

I stare down at the phone, trying to understand. The woman I've been holding in my arms is the one who has been trying to track Cadence?

I start playing back several things Ava has told me. Foster care. A friend she's worried about.

A snarl rips from my lips. She's been lying to me.

Ava sits up, clutching the covers to her chest, gripping them tightly in her hands. Her eyes are wide and her face has gone deathly pale.

My cum is leaking out of her right now. My hand balls into a fist at my side and I see her wince, curling into herself.

Even now, I force myself to relax. I would never hurt her.

"I was going to tell you," she whispers.

But I ignore her, and answer Trent instead. "Anything else?"

"Yeah," he lets out a long breath. "A woman has come forward who wants to participate in The Hunt. We've set it up for tomorrow night."

"That fast?" Normally, I carefully vet every detail of The Hunt. When done right, it's an art and a complete rewiring for the women who join. Synapsis pathways form, once done, the brain uses them over and over. But fear, it can reshape these pathways like no other emotion.

The Hunt is an opportunity for them to meaningfully change destructive patterns of behavior.

But there is too much that can go wrong, which is why I handle it myself. In this moment, I don't give a shit. Not one.

"We have several contestants who've yet to win, and are eager for another chance, which made the vetting very quick. They've all wired funds already."

My jaw clenches.

The Hunt brings in a sizable profit, but it isn't about the money.

It's also very illegal, which is why we keep it quiet.

And right now, it's a distraction I don't need. Between Ava, my father, and the selling of the casinos, I'm a little busy.

"We'll discuss it tomorrow," I grit out and then hang up the phone.

Ava is looking up at me with large, frightened eyes and it's almost enough that I want to excuse what's she's done. Almost.

My father has no love. He is a snake who would bite anything and anyone to get what he wants.

To be with a woman who would betray me…stay in my home under false pretenses… My shoulders stiffen as I glare down at her. "I have a new nickname for you, Ava. Judas."

She shakes her head wildly, her blonde hair, swinging over her back. "No. Dimitri, please." Her voice sounds so broken, it eats at me. From the first moment I saw her, something inside me understood she was mine.

That piece of me rebels now. It wants to protect. I push it back down.

"I let you into my home, to care for my daughter, and the entire time you were here, you've been deceiving me."

"I didn't know you," she cries. "All I knew was that the only family I have ever had was missing and that I would do anything to get her back."

Those words hit me. Is that not what I've been doing for my sisters?

Which is why Ava makes sense. It was her love and her loyalty that drove her. But also… "You were here to betray me, use me, and I left you with the most precious person to me in the world. My daughter."

"I wasn't here to betray you," she cries, guilt all over her face. "I just wanted to know what happened to Cadence. Find her. She's the closest thing to a sister I have."

A sob breaks from her mouth as she pulls her knees up, wrapping her arms around them and curling into a small ball.

But I pick up her clothes, tossing them on the bed next to her. "I think it's best that you sleep in your room."

"Dimitri," she says as a tear rolls down her cheek. "I was going to tell you."

"That, I find hard to believe." She's had several chances. This is the woman I picked up off the floor this morning as she completely panicked. I've given her nothing but the best of me. Fuck. I gave her my heart.

"I know you're a person I can trust. I figured that out since coming here, even with all my issues. But before I knew you, I was just trying to do anything in my power to protect Cadence."

"She doesn't need your protection," I bite back, grabbing my own underwear off the floor and yanking them up my thighs.

"Do you know where she is?" Ava tosses back the covers, moving toward me completely naked.

Her body is so beautiful bathed in moonlight that I stop, the elastic of my briefs snapping against my waist. "Is she all right?" her voice breaks as she covers her mouth with her hand, her eyes wide and pleading.

"She's fine. Better than fine. She's…" I can't tell Ava the details and I search for the words.

"But the man who answered the phone—"

I let out a string of curses. Zane shouldn't have done that.

Ava cringes away from my anger and it takes everything in me not to reach out and comfort her. Even now, I can't stand watching her hurt.

"Tomorrow, I will find a replacement for you."

I see her wince, her shoulders falling, as more tears streak down her cheeks. She wraps her arms around herself, looking away. "You don't need to do that. I'll have a replacement here by tomorrow night. I can leave now, or I can stay and help you until the replacement arrives."

There is the Ava that I fell in love with. Competent. Helpful. Vulnerable. It makes my chest ache, and it's likely why I nod instead of tossing her out of my house right now, like I should.

But I can't do it to her. She's been broken and she's trying so hard to repair herself. I know she doesn't actually know how to love.

Nor did she have a reason to trust me. But the fact that she included Anna in all of this…used my daughter to get to me. I can't abide it.

It makes me scrub my hands down my face, my feelings at war. "I wanted you to be mine."

"You don't anymore?" she whispers raw and jagged.

"No." the words sit bitter on my tongue.

"Can I at least speak to Cadence?"

"No," I shake my head. "She agreed that she'd spend three weeks with Zane and without the patterns of her old life. You'll see her in a week if she wants to return to you. If she doesn't…"

"How can I trust that?"

My jaw locks. "If you don't trust my word on this, if you think I've hurt your friend, then you don't know me at all." And that hurts because I've done nothing but try to help and heal her.

I see her cringe. "I know who you are, Dimitri. You are a man who loves his women with tenderness and compassion. But don't you also own the brothels in Las Vegas? Don't you sell women?"

My head whips back. Where did she hear that? "I give women a safe place to sell themselves. My father stuck me with that business back in Russia as a sick joke to torment me for my soft-heartedness and my desire to pursue academics rather than crime. But I've turned it around on him, using his punishment to make this world a little better. Ladies without other options flock to be under my care."

Her eyes go wide.

I likely probably shouldn't have told her any of it. This woman has been spying on me, betrayed my trust, and I'm telling her my secrets.

How could she think I'd hurt her friend? "Cadence chose to enter The Hunt and—"

"The Hunt?"

Damn. I'm frayed and I'm talking too much. She's still naked and it takes everything in me not to pull her close, run my hands over her body.

I still ache with my need for her. Instead, I reach for her tunic tank top and pull it over her head. She automatically puts her arms through the holes, obeying my silent command.

But I've struggled my entire life to heal what's been broken inside me and I can't give my affection to a woman I know doesn't have my best interests at heart.

Still, as she looks up at me, pleading, I feel myself giving in the smallest bit. Softening. She hurts and she's worried about Cadence. "I can't tell you more than that."

"Why not?"

"Because…" I sigh out. "We all sign very strict contracts for everyone's protection. But where Cadence went, she chose to go, she's safe, and she's cared for, and like you, she's trying to overcome her past."

Ava sits on the end of my bed, pulling on her leggings, her head hung low.

"You don't believe me."

"I want to," she answers. "But ever since Cadence and I have been teens, I've been bailing her out of one scrape or another. And there have been times when she's really needed me to fight for her, and this time…" She stands, pulling the pants the rest of the way up. "I know you have sisters. What would you give up if you thought they were in danger?"

"Everything," I answer, and I know the truth.

Ava *is* able to love with her whole heart. I'm just one of the many things she'd sacrifice to do it.

But my heart, deep down, still wants her.

She shakes her head and walks to the door, leaving my room without another word softly closing it behind her, the soft click sounding final.

I punch a fist into my open palm. Now that she's gone, and I' m staring at emptiness, I think I might have done that all wrong.

Her underwear is on the floor and I pick them up, balling them in my fist.

They smell like her arousal and my body betrays me as it responds. Swearing under my breath I climb into my bed.

I can't have a woman who'd lie to me. Use my daughter to get to me. I can't.

I've had too much betrayal in my life to trust a woman who would lie and deceive me like that.

But as I go to bed, her underwear is still in my hand.

# CHAPTER EIGHTEEN

Ava

I'm exhausted after not sleeping last night but I still lie awake half the night, crying into my pillow.

At three in the morning, I finally abandon the attempt and get out of bed. Drawing in a breath, I open my door and pad out to the kitchen to get a drink of water.

I move silently, feeling awkward about leaving my room.

Dimitri was clear, I'm no longer welcome here and it feels strange to move about his house. I go in the kitchen and get a glass of water, taking a few sips as I return to the safety of my room.

But that's when I hear Anna cry. She's doing much better, but I'm worried her ear is hurting her in the night. I only hesitate for a second before I open her door. "It's all right, sweetheart," I croon as she sits up in her bed, holding out her arms to me.

Lifting her up, I settle her on my hip. "Is your ear hurting?"

"Yeah," she cries into my shoulder.

"Let's get you some medicine." I carry her into the bathroom, uncapping the bottle and pouring out the dose.

She drinks it down and then burrows down deeper into me. Sighing, I snuggle her back.

Then, I carry her out into the living room, settling into the recliner. I think we'll both sleep better in the chair, her because she's up, me because the only thing better than snuggling her is sleeping against her dad.

I sigh as I think of Dimitri. He has every right to be angry with me. He trusted me with his child, and all the reasons I came here, the ones I was so sure of, have become gray and muddled.

This would all be so much easier if I could just speak to Cadence. Straighten everything out. I'm ready to listen and, thanks to Dimitri, I'd go into the conversation with an open mind. Really hear what she needs to heal. I get that I wasn't doing that before. My need to take care of her, was as much for me as it was for her. My own way of not facing my issues. But I'm ready to examine my past too.

Though I have a feeling the answer to me getting over my shit just kicked me out of his house. I close my eyes, Anna's weight relaxing against me.

I hold her tighter, kissing the top of her head. "You're wonderful, sweet Anna. Even if I never get to see you again, I just want you to know, that you've made me realize I want to have a baby of my own."

I sigh into her hair. I really am going to have to get over my issues and get married for that, though. If I'm having a baby, that little boy or girl will have two parents. I could never risk a child being left alone in the world like I was.

Before I drift off to sleep, my last thought is that I'm going to have to find a way to properly apologize to Dimitri.

I doubt he'll let me stay, but he has helped me tremendously. I can't end it like this. I have to tell him how I feel and what he's taught me even if that breaks my heart.

I don't know how long I'm asleep, but I wake to the feeling that I'm being watched.

Anna is still asleep on my chest, but as I open my eyes, I find Dimitri standing over me, his arms crossed.

He's in nothing but the boxer briefs I left him in last night.

"Her ear hurt," I whisper. My eyes close again. I'm tired and comfortable.

Dimitri's hand skims along my bare leg. "I didn't make a mistake, trusting you with my daughter, did I?"

"I would never let anything hurt her."

"How can I trust that?"

I shake my head. "I've been having that same issue. How can I trust what I see in you with what I know in my heart?"

"Fair," he replies squatting down next to me, his hand settling on my thigh.

"But I am sorry," I whisper. "You were right about some things and I…"

"Milaya," he rumbles out and a bubble rises in my chest. He's calling me sweetheart?

"Yes?" I ask, hopefully.

He pushes up, then slides his arms under me, pulling both me and Anna out of the chair.

"What are you doing?"

"We're all sleeping in my bed," he answers.

"Dimitri," I start.

"We can talk more later. And I'm still furious. But I can't sleep, and I've got to work tomorrow."

I snuggle down in his arms. "You're right. This is a good idea."

"Tomorrow, we're going to talk."

"We can talk now."

"No." He walks into his room. "I just want some sleep, and you need yours."

"Good enough for me." I am in no position to argue. He sets me lightly on the bed, Anna still in my arms, then slides behind me, snuggling me into the curve of his body.

Pressed between them, I instantly relax into the embrace, falling back to sleep.

I don't wake again until Anna does. With sleepy eyes, I look at the clock, realizing it's after nine.

"Morning," Anna chirps with a smile.

"Your ear feeling better?"

"Yep," she answers, scooting to the edge of the bed and sliding off.

"Where are you going?"

"To play."

I start to push up to follow, when Dimitri's arm tightens around me. "Where are you going?"

Smiling, I look back at him. "To watch your daughter."

"She'll be all right for a minute." And then he nuzzles my neck.

I'm not completely sure why he's so snuggly but I don't really want to question it either. I slide my hand over his arm, tilting my head to give him more access to my neck.

I tangle my legs in his. His free hand splays out on my belly. "You feel so good."

"So do you," I breathe out.

"Ava," Anna calls from the other room. "Come play."

I groan as Dimitri laughs in my neck. "You're being called."

"I hear it." I nip at my lip. The idea of not being part of Anna's life stiffens my muscles. "Is she going to be really upset when I leave?" I feel my breath catch as Dimitri's fist balls against my stomach.

"Ava," he rumbles into the skin of my neck. "I should have—"

"I've got Gertrude coming tonight."

"Gertrude?"

"The nanny."

He sighs but doesn't stiffen away. "Right."

"I can't cancel her again, she'll quit." I take a breath. I'm enjoying the snuggles and I don't really want to disrupt the harmony. But thoughts about what is coming today have started creeping in and I've never been good about ignoring those.

He pushes up on an elbow, looking down at me. "I should have known that a woman like you would take my fit of temper to heart."

"Who can blame you? And wasn't I supposed to?" My breath catches as he looks away.

"Yes." It's his turn to sigh. "And no."

My brows lift as I wait for him to explain. His hand slides over my hip. “I don’t know how to explain this, but from the first moment I met you, I just knew you were mine.”

My mouth falls open. “You’re serious.”

He kisses my neck again. “I know it’s very early in our relationship and I told you to leave my house yesterday, but seeing you with my daughter…” I feel him grimace against my neck. “I know where you belong, milaya, and it’s with us.”

I feel it too. Being in Dimitri’s life is the best thing that’s happened to me. “I want that too,” I whisper faintly. “So much.”

His warm breath rushes over my sensitive skin. “But we’re going to have to work on trust.”

“Understood,” I answer faintly. “I’ll get my stuff together, clear out the room for Gertrude. I can bring it all home later—”

“Your home is here.” He’s kissing a trail down my shoulder and over my arm.

But I push up to look back at him. “There is only one guest room. And I’m sure you want Gertrude to stay there.”

“I do. Which is why you should move your things in here.”

My mouth falls open. He can’t be serious. “Yesterday…”

“I know what I said,” he says as his eyes hold mine. “You’re right. You couldn’t have known what kind of man I am. But Anna…”

“I would never have hurt her in any way.”

“I understand, milaya, and I trust you with her care.”

For a moment, emotion overwhelms me. His acceptance and understanding fill my heart in ways I can barely describe. I push up from the bed. “Thank you.”

“Where are you going?” He sits up too, his brow puckering into a frown.

“I’m going to go play with Anna.”

He cocks his head to the side as he looks back at me.

“Because, whatever I hoped to find out by being here, I have always been clear that Anna deserves the best.”

He pushes up too, pulling me in his arms and dropping his mouth to mine in a kiss that devours and claims.

There is no fear, though, only red-hot desire as I wrap my arms around his neck and kiss him back.

I want everything he has to give and I'm not going to let my past keep me from living the best kind of future.

Which is what Cadence has been trying to tell me for a while. I ease back. "I...I know I can't speak to Cadence, but can you deliver a message for me?"

He lifts his head too. "Ava—"

"I need her to know that I finally understand what she was trying to tell me. And I'm ready to move forward in my life and that..." I take in a long breath, the next words difficult. "That I understand if she can't have me in hers anymore. I love her enough to let her go if that's what she needs." My throat closes on the last words, emotion making my chest tight.

"Oh, milaya," he leans down then, his nose touching one cheek as his palm holds the other. "You love her with your whole heart."

"I know I got some stuff wrong, but..."

He trails kisses along my jaw. "You got loads right, and don't worry. We're going to learn to love together."

"You need to learn to love?"

"My father was not the best example. I'm not actually certain he can love anyone, but himself. It's difficult to be raised by someone like that. I have to quiet his voice in my head always to listen to my heart. I'm getting better."

I nod, even as he kisses that spot behind my ear.

"Ava," Anna calls from the doorway, her little brow slashed into a line. "Come."

I smile, a little laugh making my chest vibrate. "Feeling better this morning, my little lamb?"

"Yes. Come." She holds up her chubby little hand, waving me forward.

I kiss Dimitri's neck before I move out of the circle of his arms.

He watches me go. "Fifteen minutes and then you have a date with me in the shower."

My eyes go wide as a flush of color washes down my chest.

A shower with him sounds amazing.

# CHAPTER NINETEEN

Dimitri

It's the most pleasant morning with Anna and Ava flitting about the house, laughing and making noise.

My daughter loves Ava as much as I do.

Which means, Anna is proving to be my greatest competition for Ava's attention.

It takes me longer than fifteen minutes to get Ava into the shower. Anna needs breakfast and more play time.

But by the time I turn on the hot spray, I know it's just a matter of time before we're interrupted again.

Which is why I pull Ava into my arms, lifting her feet off the ground. She gets the message and wraps her legs around my waist, allowing me to instantly sink inside of her willing body.

She feels so good wrapped around my cock, that I groan, burying my face in the crook of her neck.

She's so open to me, her head tilting to give me access, even as a flood of her juices soak me along with the spray. I'd like to stay here all day, but this one is going to have to be quick.

Which is why I grab her hips, lifting her off me before pulling her back down, making us both moan.

I set a spanking pace, working her up and down my cock as her legs flex around my waist to make it even faster, harder until we're both panting.

She feels so good, so right, I know, this is exactly where I'm meant to be. I spread my feet wide, fucking her harder as she arches back, her chest thrusting out, her cries and gasps increasing in intensity so that I know she's close.

I can feel my own orgasm building, the cum boiling in my balls as I hold out a little longer. I won't cum until she does, but I'm strung so taut, I feel like I could break.

I push through, her legs locking around my waist as her hands dig into my shoulders, her fingernails surely leaving divots in my skin.

Finally, she breaks, her cry filling the bathroom. It's my cue to let go, a flood of cum filling her as a guttural roar rips from my chest.

I collapse against the wall, still holding her in my arms. I'm a man with stamina but the sex with Ava is some other level of fulfilling and draining.

She's complete mush in my arms, her body melded to mine. "That was amazing."

I chuckle, kissing along her shoulder. "Yes. It was."

Her head lolls back against the shower wall. "I think I might be ready for missionary."

That instantly infuses me with energy, my cock stiffening inside her. "We've got plenty of time to get there, and I've got lots of creative options until we do."

I feel her smile as she lowers one leg to the ground, her toe dancing on the wet tile. "Good to know."

I think she's starting to understand that I mean for this to be a long-term arrangement. I trace her sides as she brings the other leg down, supporting her own weight.

"We can take as long as you need, milaya." I cup her ass, pulling her hips back into the cradle of mine.

"Thank you, Dimitri. And thanks for understanding about..." Her hand lifts, waving in the air.

"I'll get your message to Cadence."

"Thank you." I hear the choke in her voice.

We wash, get out of the shower and get dressed. Ava leaves me to my work while she returns to Anna's room.

The new nanny is coming late this afternoon. But if I have my way, Ava isn't going anywhere. She's moving into my room. And with a nanny here, we can take much longer showers.

Picking up my phone, I dial Zane.

We carefully vet contestants for The Hunt and Zane was the man I'd hoped would win Cadence.

He's got loads of dominant strength, but a balanced temperament that would be patient and kind enough to understand that Cadence would need a steady hand and love instead of force.

"Dimitri?" Zane answers, sounding leery. Though, Trent does call both of them regularly to make certain everyone is safe, a call from me is...unexpected. The couple is supposed to be left alone.

"Everything going all right?" I ask, leaning back in my chair. "How is the cabin?"

"It's hardly a cabin. And yes. Everything is fine. Which is what I told Trent when he called yesterday."

My mouth twitches, knowing I've been caught. "Good. I'm calling you instead of Cadence out of respect."

"Respect for...?"

"The Hunt. The process..." I take a breath. "But I've got Cadence's friend Ava in my house and she's trying to do some healing of her own."

"Cadence doesn't want to speak to Ava," Zane rumbles, sounding like a man ready to fight for his woman. Good.

"That's why I'm calling you instead of her."

"Go ahead."

"Ava says that she's ready to accept Cadence leaving her life if that is the way for Cadence to heal. She just wants confirmation that Cadence is safe. That's it."

"You can't give that to her?"

"I've tried, but it's a matter of trust, and considering I'm the man who organized The Hunt, she's been struggling to take me at my word."

Zane grunts. He must mute the phone because it goes silent. I hear nothing but silence for a minute, longer, then he comes back. "She's going to call Ava. Just for a minute."

I let out a long breath. It breaks the rules, and I know Trent has trackers on their phones, so he'll know that I've called Zane, and that Cadence called Ava, but I'll explain it to him later.

"Thanks, Zane." I hang up, striding out of my office and to Anna's room, where I find Anna and Ava snuggled up together, playing with the doll house.

It makes my chest tight to see them and I almost hate to interrupt. But Ava needs this. "Ava, do you have your phone?"

"Yes. Why?"

But her phone rings a moment later. She pulls it out of her pocket, her eyes going wide.

I give her a soft smile. I know how badly she needed this moment and I'm so glad to give it to her.

# CHAPTER TWENTY

AVA

THE SIGHT of Cadence's name on my phone sends a jolt of shock coursing through me. Kissing Anna's head, I stand up and hit the answer button, my heart pounding in my chest. "Hello."

"Hey," Cadence answers.

My free hand comes to my face, covering my eyes as relief wars with anger, love, and resentment. "You're all right."

"I'm fine," she sighs.

My mouth opens as words crowd my mouth. *How could you do this to me?* first on the list of things I'd like to say. But I swallow the words, remembering what I told Dimitri about letting Cadence go. "I'm glad."

"I'm sorry I left without a word. I didn't think you'd understand." Listening to her words, I swallow down another lump as I fight for control. Dimitri wraps his arms around me, and lifts me off the floor, carrying me from Anna's room.

"You're right. I didn't." I still don't. I guess I never understood half of what Cadence did growing up. But today isn't the day for that. I made a promise to Dimitri that I would accept her leaving my life if only I could get confirmation that she was safe. "I'm glad you're all right."

"You're okay?" she asks back.

"I'm fine, Cade. I'll be fine..." My throat closes and I press my forehead against Dimitri's neck, my eyes squeezing closed. "I wish you the best."

"Ava," she says in a rush of air. "Don't say it like that. Like you don't want me anymore."

"I think it's you who doesn't want me, Cadence. And that's all right. I want you to be happy. I always have."

"Shit," she mutters. "It has nothing to do with you. Yes, you need to get out there and take some risks and really live life, but I'm the one who has been dragging you down. You just didn't see it. And I'm trying to get right so that I can be the friend you need instead of the selfish black hole who sucks up all your resources."

She draws in a desperate, unsteady breath, before she speaks again. "I knew if I said that to you, you'd tell me I wasn't, and that you didn't mind helping me. But you should, Ava. You're way better to me than I deserve. Sometimes I seem angry because, I know I'm not just fucking up my life but yours too."

Tears start leaking down my cheeks. "I'd go to hell for you, Cadence. You're not a black hole. You're not fucking up my life. You're my family. The only person who has ever protected me in this crazy ass world. I've always needed you as much or more than you needed me."

"Shit," she chokes on her own tears. "I messed this up again, didn't I?"

"It's fine. I forgive you. Do what you need to do, and then, maybe we can go to couples counseling or something."

For a moment there is a pause and then she bursts out laughing. "For real?"

"I went to one. A counselor. You were right. Five minutes in and I ended up on the floor with a panic attack. I clearly need some help. I'm going to go back. Try to solve these intimacy issues I'm carrying..."

"Ava," Cadence gasps. "Were you telling her about Hank?"

"You know I don't like saying his name."

"I should have stabbed that fucker seven more times."

"That's enough," a man rumbles in the background. "I can hear you getting worked up."

"This is different, Zane. I'm allowed to be violent when someone I love is being attacked."

My limbs turn to jelly. "I love you too."

"I'm glad we talked," she whispers. "I don't know how you managed to get me on the phone with all the rules."

"It's a long story but the juicy part is that I started dating." Dimitri finally lowers my feet to the floor, my body sliding down his. I smile into Dimitri's chest.

Cadence pauses. "Shut up."

"Yep. Can't wait to tell you."

"Same. Same. We'll talk in a week when I'm back." There is a pause. Part of me, even now, doesn't want to hang up the phone, can't let her go again.

But it's time I stopped hanging on so tightly. "Bye, Cadence. Good luck. I love you."

"You too, Ava. Sleep tight."

I smile, remembering the words we'd whisper to each other because we didn't have a mother to say them. I want to say more, but instead I hang up the phone.

Dimitri holds me tightly, not saying a word. I let the silence fill the space between us, so glad for the comfort of his arms.

I'd like to be mad at Cadence, but her leaving was the push I needed to find myself here. "I think I might be in love with you."

His hands spread out on my back. "Good."

"Good?" I lift my face to look up at him. "That's it?"

"No. But it would be awkward to be married to me if you weren't. I tried that once, it doesn't work all that well."

My brows lift. He leans down and kisses me. "What are we talking about now?"

"I love you too. You are my future, Ava Tantor."

"Oh," I flush, my hands resting on his chest. "That's lovely."

He leans down and kisses me then. "I want to marry you."

"Oh," I repeat. "That's fast."

He chuckles, before his eyes grow more serious, narrowing. "Don't worry. You've got plenty of time to consider. I've got a few issues to work through as well while you do."

"You've got issues?" From my perspective, he's got careful control of both his life and his feelings.

"My father doesn't allow me access to my sisters. They are trapped in a prison of his cruelty."

"That's awful," I gasp out, my hands lightly massaging his neck.

"I'm forcing his hand, which means I'm poking a very large bear. I know you need time, and so do I. As soon as I've rescued my sisters, we can discuss the future again."

I push up on tiptoe and kiss his lips. It doesn't surprise me he's trying to rescue more women. Dimitri is a man who cares for the women he loves, body, mind, and soul.

I pull back a few inches, meeting his gaze again. "Can you tell me more?"

Holding my face, he kisses me again. "I'll tell you all of it. But for today, let's just focus on you. Tomorrow, we can discuss my messed-up family and my narcissistic and sadistic father."

I wince on his behalf. Because we have this in common. Really messed-up pasts. No wonder he understands me.

And for the first time since I met him, Cadence is no longer between us. I'm free to just enjoy him.

Which makes my stomach twist in fear.

If life has taught me one thing, it's that moments like these carry a very heavy cost. At least for people like me, the second I relax, something terrible is about to happen…

# CHAPTER TWENTY-ONE

Ava

Gertrude arrives at five. The meet and greet with Dimitri goes well enough. He's polite, welcoming.

Gertrude still gives him the side eye.

She's a crusty old lady, and I could blame her standoffishness on that. But the way she eyes the tattoos on his hands, it's clear that she's skeptical about what kind of man she's moving in with.

I wonder how she's going to react when she realizes I'm also part-time living here, even after she moves in.

I wince, trying to remember the HR policy for finding nannies for friends and family. I shake my head. It's a problem for tomorrow.

Tonight, it's my job to get Gertrude settled and to help Anna adjust. It's been a lot of changes for her, and I don't want her to be upset.

Dimitri leaves in the evening for work. Just before he goes, he kisses me goodbye. "Tonight, I'll be late."

We make dinner, play, watch her favorite show, before I walk Gertrude through the bedtime routine.

Sitting on the couch, Gertrude works on her knitting while I fire up my laptop, intent upon finding Gertrude's permanent replacement for Anna's nanny. No more dragging my feet.

I've set up a few interviews for next week, but I need to get a few more scheduled. And then there are the pile of new requests I've been ignoring.

I sigh, as I open my email, and start sifting through all the unanswered correspondence. It's going to take me weeks to catch up.

That's when my cell phone rings. I don't recognize the number, and I squint down at the local number before I pick up. "Hello?"

"Miss Tantor, it's Henry from the front desk."

"Oh. Hi, Henry."

"Mister Trent is here to see you."

"Mister Trent?" My brow furrows in momentary confusion.

"He's here often, ma'am. He works with Mr. Ivanov. He's got a key, but he asked me to call up as a courtesy."

My eyes widen as I make the connection. "Of course. Send him up." I close my laptop again, nipping at my lip as I set it on the coffee table, and get up to start moving toward the kitchen.

Just as I reach it, the elevator opens.

A man dressed in all black steps out of the elevator. He's Dimitri's age, I think, though far grayer, but no less distinguished, his clothes finely cut, his hair perfectly coiffed. He's handsome enough and sporting a friendly smile. "You must be Ava." His Russian accent is laced with a tension I don't quite understand.

"I am. Trent?" For some reason, I don't reach out my hand. I don't want to touch him…maybe I'm not as healed as I thought.

"Yes, that's right." His smile widens, revealing more of his teeth. "Dimitri actually sent me to collect you."

"Collect me?" My brow furrows. "What does that mean?"

He runs a hand through his salt-and-pepper hair, the smile disappearing. Dropping his hand, he pulls at the lapels of his coat. "I don't want you to be concerned, but Cadence fell this evening and she's been brought to a local hospital."

I gasp, my hands flying to my mouth. "You're serious?"

"I'm afraid so. She's asking for you and so Dimitri sent me to take you to her so that you can see each other."

My hands drop, clasping by my chest. "Is she all right? How seriously is she hurt?"

"She's going to be fine. Hurt her leg, but we all thought you'd want to visit. Check in on her." I don't need to hear any more. Spinning, I race into the other room, grabbing my sweatshirt and slipping on my sneakers. "I'll be back, Gert. There's been an emergency," I call to Gertrude as I finish putting on my second shoe.

She looks up at me with concern, but I don't give her time to ask questions as I stand back up and race back toward the kitchen.

As soon as Trent sees me, he pushes the button for the elevator.

It isn't until we're closed in the space that I realize, I'm going to be alone with a man who isn't Dimitri.

It's just one of those things I don't do.

I breathe through the panic, knowing that I have to control it for Cadence's sake, but my legs are wobbly as we reach the garage.

It helps that Trent's car is parked where Dimitri's usually is, and that, with a press of his phone, Trent is opening the garage gate.

Clearly, Trent is a man whom Dimitri trusts. I take a few cleansing breaths as I climb into the car with him.

He pulls the car out of the garage, moving through the Vegas streets to the highway.

The traffic is thick enough that for a while we don't speak. Instead, I stare out the window, lost in thoughts of Cadence, our past, and of Dimitri.

Trent lets me sink into my own thoughts, and I relax, the silence a comfort.

But as the traffic thins, I realize, I have no idea where we're going. "Where is the hospital? I thought it was local?"

"South," he answers.

"The hospital that Cadence was taken to is south?" I ask, his one-word answer making me uneasy again.

"And I meant it was local to her." He looks over at me, but that does little to calm me.

In fact, his sidelong glance makes my chest grow tight. "And where is that?" As the highway slips by, all that I can see is open desert.

"Not far now. There's a small, forested area that's fed by a river. We have cabins there that we use for The Hunt."

"The Hunt," I repeat, a tingle of dread moving down my spine. Dimitri was very specific that he couldn't share details. I'm surprised that Trent mentions it at all.

"After The Hunt, we like to have a quick place for the winner and the prize to go."

"The winner? The prize?" I don't like my friend being referred to as a prize. I look over at him, clasping my hands to stop them from shaking. Why is he telling me this? And why am I just parroting back key words?

"The women volunteer. Most of them are like Cadence, they struggle to build meaningful relationships in the outside world and are looking for a way to disrupt their own patterns. A neural reset of patterned thinking if you will. A way to break their cycle of behavior. Dimitri could tell you more about it."

"Dimitri knows about neural resets?"

Trent gives me a knowing stare accompanied with a smirk. "Did he not tell you? I'm not surprised. The two of you don't know each other that well and you did betray him."

A drum beats in my chest as the blood rushes in my ears.

"Dimitri studied neurobiology before his father forced him to quit and join the family business. But he uses the knowledge he acquired to change the lives of so many women. Something about the fear response helps create new neural pathways better than any other response. If you ask me, he's attempting to rewrite his mother's ending, but it makes sense I'd think that. I studied psychology."

I stare at him, hardly able to catch my breath as the shaking takes over my whole body. Any other time, I'd enjoy the tidbit I've just learned about Dimitri but in this moment, I can only think of my friend. "Cadence did this? She allowed a man to hunt her? Capture her?"

"Not man. Men. Five of them. Zane was the winner."

"That's not how she was hurt?" I cry, fumbling to pull out my phone and call Dimitri. Somehow, I just need to hear his voice to assure me I haven't stepped into danger. Because this has started to feel...crazy.

But Trent plucks the phone from my hand before I've even processed what he's doing.

I let out a small cry. "That's my phone!"

He doesn't answer. Instead, he rolls down the window and tosses the phone out of the moving car.

I whip my head around, seeing the lit screen as the phone lands on the tar, bouncing a few times before it comes to a stop. I watch until it goes dark, my throat closing as I clutch the back of my seat.

I've made that mistake before, thinking that a man attacking me was all just a misunderstanding. There is no mistake here, and no point in asking for more information. Trent is not telling me his motivations.

I draw in a jagged gulp, trying to calm my spinning thoughts as the blood rushes in my ears.

I wrap my arms around my middle. "Where are we really going?" I just manage to whisper through ragged gasps.

"The Hunt," he answers with a sneer. "You are the next prize."

"No." But my voice isn't much more than a whisper. I can hardly make it work.

"And by the way, a man claims the prize by fucking her. On the ground in the dirt, or against a tree for any of the other players to watch."

I curl into a ball, the very idea of men fighting, one of them brutally taking me, makes my brain go white and then black.

# CHAPTER TWENTY-TWO

Dimitri

"Trent is late," I look down at my watch and then grimace at the five men in front of me. If I'd been paying more attention the last few days, I would have never agreed to this line-up of fighters.

We have applicants by the hundreds, but I'm very careful about whom I accept. They are men of the strongest variety. Soldiers, fighters, stockbrokers, all top of their field and all looking for a deep, meaningful connection with a woman the modern world makes difficult.

The women who participate want the same. A true protector and provider. But I am careful to pair each female with the right contestants.

In Cadence's case, the men were all of seemingly balanced temperament, to make certain they'd be patient with her struggles. When she doesn't trust, she fights.

Her Hunt required players that would not use force with her, only on other men. It was imperative. Of course, one hunter managed to fool me, a mistake I promised myself I would not make again.

Which is why the players of this field fill me with alarm. This lineup is twenty times more aggressive than Cadence's. All of these men have competed before, most of them in the most aggressive manner possible.

I don't like it. I'm not sure I'd allow any of them a second chance to compete. The fact that they're all here on one hunt has me seriously questioning Trent's judgment. And now, he's late.

I've never doubted Trent before, we're brothers in arms and in pain. But lately, he's been acting strangely. Trent was one of my father's top guys before we came to the states. My father blackmailed him, much the way he did me, taking the woman that Trent loved in order to force Trent's loyalty.

But Trent has been faithfully helping me take power away from my father so that we can get his wife, and my sisters, back.

The men flanking me shift restlessly.

We're in the middle of a field, a river winding on the left, trees ringing us on all other sides. The river has created a forested oasis. Which is why I chose this spot. It's close enough to Vegas to be convenient, but quiet and private enough that our activities are not discovered.

I bought the area and fenced it with a twelve-foot wall to keep prying eyes out.

"What the fuck?" One of them rumbles. Tazz. Crazy MMF fighter who likes spirited women. His last girlfriend was the CFO of a major company. He's quite gentle with women, it's other men with whom he's inappropriately hostile. His aggression was a problem during the last round of The Hunt.

"Calm your shit down," Callum rumbles. He's ex-Special Forces and scared the woman in his competition so much that she spent the first week with her winner, curled around him like a fly stuck to fly paper. He didn't mind, and it likely helped their bond, but it was unnecessary for Callum to frighten her that much.

I look down the line of them, my eyes narrowing. Trent knew I'd flagged each of these fighters. Why are they here? He'd never make a decision like this without speaking to me. Why did he do so this time?

Which makes my skin prickle with warning. Trent has been straight-up acting strange and I would have noticed if I wasn't so distracted.

My muscles twitch as I pull out my phone and call him. He doesn't pick up.

But I understand why he didn't answer in a moment when headlights flash through the trees, and I hear the clang of the gate closing. He's finally here.

I hope he picked a woman who is prepared for this level of masculine energy. It's going to take a strong woman to survive this.

He kills the headlights and the path from the parking area to the field goes dark again.

The air stills and I feel its crackle as the men around me shift restlessly, ready to begin.

I've checked all the contestants for weapons, but I reach back feeling my own pistol where it's nestled in the small of my back. I look to the right, one of my men standing at the end of the line.

Alex. He looks back with the same wariness that I feel.

The entire place is rigged with cameras, more of my men are in a booth watching in case they need to intervene. We have all sorts of safety measures in place, but that doesn't stop the sizzle of wariness that zips through my body.

I grab the walkie talkie from my hip, hitting the call button as I bark into the receiver. "What's Trent doing?"

The line crackles as one of the men answers, "Leading the girl to the field now. Hunt should start any second." I don't recognize the voice on the other end which only heightens my concerns. Something is very wrong.

The contestants have heard his words and they still, ready and waiting.

The air crackles with their tension and mine as my back molars grind together.

Looking toward the path, a lone figure appears, small and hunched. My eyes narrow. She's wrong. I know it in a single glance.

A woman with this sort of field should be a fighter. The kind of strong who can handle the aggression. This woman is frightened out of her wits. "Wait," I rumble low even as Tazz takes a step forward, muscles twitching.

Alex steps forward too and the other men follow suit, shaking their limbs as they prepare, waiting for the sound of the horn. "Wait," I yell out and then hit the button on the walkie talkie. "Do not sound the horn. I repeat, do not sound—"

There is no answer, no one responds before the horn blasts through the field, my command ignored.

The woman screams and something in the pitch of her voice, I hear the fear.

But also…

The tone. It takes a half second for me to process and then I know. It's Ava. Ava stands on the other end of this field.

My body springs into action before my mind catches up, and I take off at a full sprint. I reach Alex first. "They can't reach the woman," I grit out. "Stop them at any cost."

Then, I push forward to the first contestant.

I've been trained since childhood to be a fighter, and I don't hesitate now. I jab my fingers into the side of his throat. My attack is unexpected, he goes down like a ton of bricks.

The thunder of the other men's feet keeps them from hearing, and I keep the element of surprise.

Ahead of me, Ava has curled into the fetal position on the ground. It pushes my legs faster, as I reach another of the hunters, hitting him in the kidney with a blow that sends him falling to the ground. He'll recover and then he'll be behind me, but my first job is to get to Ava before any other man.

I reach the next man and swipe out a leg, tripping him and sending him crashing to the ground. I hear the crack of bone as he hits the ground, but I don't look back.

There are only two men in front of me: Tazz and Callum.

Tazz veers to his right, knocking into the other man with such force, that Callum flies to the side, landing with a thud in the grass.

I grit my teeth and pump my legs faster, air burning my chest. My best move is to push him hard right before he reaches her and then stand guard as any able fighter makes his second attack.

Tazz snarls as he looks over his shoulder, meeting my eye. And then with a burst of speed, he pulls away.

I roar rips from my chest as I push my body harder, my lungs near bursting from the effort.

But that's when a figure in black steps from the shadows. For a moment fear beats like a drum in my chest. I'm losing ground and now there is another man…

The dark figure sends a fist flying through the air, the punch landing with deadly accuracy on Tazz's jaw. He stops mid stride, dropping like a stone.

That's when I meet the eyes of the man in black.

Killian Smith.

I don't have a moment to consider what that might mean as I draw closer to Ava. I slow my speed, pulling up and spinning my legs landing on either side her where she's curled in the fetal position on the ground. "Ava," I push out of my bursting lungs, barely able to say the words. "It's me."

She looks up at me her blue eyes looking…haunted. And then, she's wrapping herself around my leg, locked so tight, I'm not sure I can even fight.

But her touch, it clears my head, my body infused with adrenaline as I prepare to protect my woman.

Two of the other fighters surge toward us a I turn to face them, but Killian steps between me and them. "If you want to live through the next five minutes…" He pulls two pistols from his belt. "I'd suggest you stop."

The other fighters instantly obey, and for a split second, I let out a breath of relief. But that's when I hear the click of a gun next to my temple. "Sorry, Dimitri, but you don't get to keep her."

Trent.

The barrel presses into my skin.

I'm going to kill him slowly.

# CHAPTER TWENTY-THREE

Ava

I can't think, can't breathe, as I hold on to Dimitri. How he ever reached me, the miracle of it, I can't even begin to understand, but I'm not sure I care. They'll have to kill me before I let go of his leg.

Which feels like a distinct possibility as I hear the click of a gun's hammer. I jolt against Dimitri. His response? He drops a light hand on the top of my head, his fingers massaging my scalp.

"Sorry, Dimitri, but you're going to have to hand over the girl."

"I don't think so," Dimitri answers, his fingers not changing tempo, just continuing their light strokes. My fingers dig into his thigh as though I'm preparing for an onslaught. My grip is so tight, I'm likely bruising his skin.

This is my worst nightmare.

Five men running at me with the intent of forcibly taking me. I grip Dimitri even tighter. He promised me no one would ever hurt me.

In this moment, I cling to that promise exactly like I cling to his leg.

"You don't have a choice."

"Oh, but he does…" the man in black answers. If Dimitri is frightening with his tattoos, this man…

He truly looks like the devil. Dark hair and eyes and the sharp sort of locks that add this sinister air to his appearance.

He swings one of the two pistols around, pointing at Dimitri or Trent. I can't be sure. "You can try…" he drawls in this emotionally detached voice that makes the hair on my neck stand up. "But you'll never make it to your Porsche."

"You think you can stop a Russian?" Trent spits.

"Me alone? Probably. Yeah. But my four brothers are waiting for you just in case I don't." The man in black replies, sounding equal parts bored and confident.

Trent lowers the gun a foot, a grimace pulling at his mouth.

But the man in black isn't finished speaking. "Just so we're all on the same page, Dimitri, he betrayed you and sold you out to your father, to get his Anastasia returned. Jake tapped his phone."

"I had already puzzled all that out," Dimitri answers with a quiet calm that helps my arms relax. Dimitri doesn't sound worried, his touch remaining light. I tilt my head up to look at him, his fingers stroking through my hair.

"I had no choice," Trent rumbles, baring his teeth. "Your father made that clear."

He doesn't look down, his gaze fixed on Trent. "Where is he?"

"I don't know."

Dimitri makes a small snarling noise. "You had better be lying, because if you're not, you're a fool."

"You ought to understand," Trent fires back, his voice taking on a snarl. "Anastasia is the love of my life."

Dimitri's jaw goes rock hard. "I do. But I also know that I'd never sacrifice another person's loved one for my own goals. I'd just fight harder."

Trent roars. "I tried to protect you. Telling you about her spying and her deceit. She betrayed you. You should let her go, trade her for your sisters, while your father still thinks she holds value to you."

Blood roars in my ears. Would Dimitri do that? Would he trade me for them? My eyes squeeze shut and a small sob breaks from my lips as I realize the men hunting me was not my worst nightmare.

This is.

The idea that the person I let past my defenses won't love me back. That I'm too broken, not lovable. This is why I've hidden myself away all this time. Clung to Cadence.

Because letting another person in, it opens me to experience the hurt all over again.

Dimitri's fingers move from my scalp, down to my jaw, the tips lightly dancing over my skin. "Hush, milaya," he whispers into the night. "You're safe with me."

I look up at him, so strong and tall, his jaw set in a resolute line. And I just know…

I can trust Dimitri.

I press my cheek to the inside of his thigh. Dimitri has always been a man of principle. Even before my mind could believe it, I felt it deep in my heart.

He'll do everything in his power to keep me safe.

And there isn't anything I wouldn't give to him. By his side is where I am meant to be.

I hear the thundering footsteps of more men, and I freeze in fear once again, my grip growing impossibly tight on Dimitri's leg.

Just like always, his hand remains gentle.

"Those would be my guards," Trent crosses his arms over his chest. "You didn't think I'd do this alone, did you? You will give up the girl in exchange for Anastasia and your sisters It's a good deal and you should be thanking me."

The massive man who'd been on the ground, the one who almost reached me stands up, his hand rubbing over his jaw. "What's wrong with your woman?"

"Wrong?" Dimitri asks.

"Get back on the ground," Trent spits, swinging the gun toward the other man's chest.

The rough fighter ignores Trent and looks down at me.

"She was victimized," the tattooed man with the guns answers.

Dimitri makes a noise deep in his throat. "How do you know that?"

"My wife has some of the same behaviors."

Wife? That man is married? He looks too scary. Then again, looks can be deceiving.

I open my eyes to look at him. His gaze meets mine and I swear, I see warmth in his eyes. "But don't you worry, Ava," he calls, sounding calm and reassuring. "They'll have to get through me and I'm devilishly difficult to take down."

A small squeak comes out of my throat.

The other fighter steps closer, his shoulders expanding as he stares back at Trent. How is this the group of men where I have found real champions? Men willing to stand up and protect me. Warriors. That's what they are.

A realization fires through me. Real strength, real masculinity protects, it doesn't harm. Which means, maybe Cadence's plan wasn't quite so crazy after all.

The other fighter, the one who'd been hunting me moments before, takes another step to stand at Dimitri's side. "I'll stand with you."

"Price?"

"I'd like to compete next time for free." The fighter speaks like they're bargaining for a used car, not a life-or-death situation.

"Done." Dimitri answers.

Another man, also in black, steps out of the woods. I only have a moment to wonder if this is friend of foe when the devil rumbles, "Tris."

"Don't start, Killian." He comes to Dimitri's other side, creating a ring of men around me.

Behind Trent appears a line of guards, dressed in black, with their faces covered by bandanas. I squeeze my eyes shut again.

"Whatever Trent paid you, I'll double it," Dimitri calls to them.

"It wasn't money," Trent sneers. "Their families are safe because—"

I feel the slight jostle as the man next to Dimitri grabs at his waist, and then the sound of the gun pops. I scream, shrinking even closer to the ground.

I hear the thud and my eyes spring open again. Trent lays dead on the ground.

Shock rolls through me. I squeeze my eyes shut again, as I press my lips together to keep from screaming.

I'm surprised, I've never seen death like this. But I can't say I'm sad. That man just kidnapped me and dragged me here. The other guards shift awkwardly in a line, as though they're not certain what to do.

"Killian," Dimitri calls. "Would you be so kind as to take Ava to my car?"

"No," I whimper. "I want to be with you."

Dimitri leans closer. "Milaya, you can trust him, I promise."

"Triston will take her," Killian answers. "He scares women way less than I do and besides, he's less skilled with a pistol."

A man bends down, smiling at me with an easy grace that makes me relax. He's so handsome, he looks like a GQ model. "Hi, Ava. Triston Smith, pleasure to make your acquaintance."

How can he sound like that with a dead body a few feet away? Despite that thought, I start to relax but then realize his effect and give him a side eye. "Has anyone ever told you that you're almost too handsome?"

A laugh bursts from Killian's lips. From somewhere in the grass a man moans. One of the hunters? It stops Killian's laugh, but Tris gives me another easy smile. "Yes. All of my brothers and most of my ex-girlfriends."

"Tris," Dimitri rumbles. "Through the woods. Now, please."

Triston offers his hand and I take it, unclenching my muscles, though they don't want to work.

He reaches for me, I'm sure he's trying to help, but I lock up again with a whimper. "Hush, Ava," Dimitri says before he bends down and grabs me himself. I unlock instantly, and he lifts me up, my body naturally bending toward his. But before I can get my arms around his neck, he tosses me to Triston like I weigh nothing at all.

Triston catches me and crushes me to his chest as he sprints toward the woods.

But we've barely made it into the line of trees when the sound of more shots fills the air.

We're down in a second, Triston's body covering mine. Was he hit?

I scream, an ear-piercing noise that I can't control. It's the fear bubbling out. I know he doesn't want to hurt me, might be hurt himself, but I'm too raw. I can't control the reaction.

"Are you all right?" he rumbles, his hands coming to my ears to cover them from the noise.

Those words help penetrate the bubble of fear that controlled my mind. "I…men…" I can't get any more words out as I draw in a jagged breath.

But he only leans his head closer to mine. "I'll get you out of here. Don't worry."

I clutch at his shirt, shrinking into him.

It only takes another thirty seconds before I hear the crash of footsteps again. "Ava?"

"Dimitri," I gasp.

Triston lifts his head and then I catch sight of Dimitri charging toward us. "Is she hurt?"

"N-n-no," I push out. "Just scared."

Triston places a gentle hand on my face. "I wouldn't let anything happen to you, promise."

I don't have a chance to tell him that his body on top of mine, was what had me so frightened. Dimitri pushes him off of me and bends over to check, his hands running up and down my limbs as he checks for injuries. I relax into the ground, a long deep breath leaving my lungs. "Are you hurt?" I ask him.

"I'm fine, sweetheart." He runs his hands over my ribs, my stomach, before he picks me up, cradling me against his body.

I close my eyes and wrap myself around him. "How did you ever make it to me?"

"He was fueled by love," Killian calls from behind him. I expected his tone to hold mockery, but he sounds absolutely sincere.

Dimitri kisses my forehead. "He's not wrong."

I close my eyes at the feel of his warm lips against me. "What happens next?"

"The new nanny is with Anna?"

"That's right."

"In that case, I think we stay right here and wait for my father to come."

# CHAPTER TWENTY-FOUR

Dimitri

In an ideal world, Ava would be tucked safely at home with Anna. Carrying my woman, I turn to Killian. "I need you to make certain my daughter is protected."

Killian grimaces. "I can go, but then I'm not here to help you protect Ava."

I feel Ava's shiver of fear as she shakes in my arms. "Send him to Anna," she whispers anyway.

I look down at her, my heart rising into my throat. I can't even imagine how afraid she was today.

That was her worst nightmare come to life.

And even after all that, she's willingly sending Killian to protect my daughter?

I knew that when Ava loved, she'd love with her whole heart. But it steals my breath to see the proof right before my eyes.

I dip my head to kiss her, my mouth crashing into hers.

I should be gentle. She's raw and vulnerable, but she doesn't stiffen or pull away.

She kisses me back, her lips soft and pliant under mine.

Every man my father blackmailed is dead. I know it makes me a killer, but it also protects their families. Men are soldiers, it's the women and children who need to be protected.

It's a fact I've always understood.

With their deaths, my father will not seek retribution. And just like I protected those unknown wives, mothers, children, I will protect my family.

Ava and Anna will have my full protection even if it costs me my life. That is my code. And it is the code that I lead with here in Vegas.

I lift my head, looking toward the line of trees. Beyond the small patch of woods are three tiny homes equipped with all the latest comforts. They're made for after The Hunt. The place a man can take the woman he's claimed to complete their bond.

Cadence and Zane are in one of them now.

Next to me, Tazz keeps pace, bruises blooming on his jaw and cheek.

Tris already loaded the men too hurt to stay into his car to drop them at an emergency room.

But the other Smith brothers have joined us. Gris, a man who moves with the skilled confidence of a trained fighter, is to my right. Beside him, Jake and Luke Kincaid. While Jake is the head of security, Luke is the primary muscle for Kincaid Enterprises.

These men have been my rivals. Did I think I didn't like them? The fact that they are here speaks volumes about their characters. They operate under the same code as I do, and for that, they have my full allegiance.

"You're certain you don't want me here?" Killian asks. "It's where the fight is likely to happen."

"I'm certain," I nod at him. "Keep my daughter safe."

With a nod, he veers off, disappearing almost instantly into the dark. I'm half tempted to send Ava with him. But transit will be dangerous and by my side is where she belongs. I'll die before I let my father hurt her.

We enter the woods, the quiet making my senses sharpen as I search through the trees, watching and listening for danger.

Our steps slow as my head swivels back and forth.

Ava's hands tighten on my neck. I hold her closer as we traverse the narrow strip of woods between us and the cabins.

My father is coming. I have no doubt.

Trent was only the tip of the iceberg. The rest of the danger is under the water, waiting to emerge.

The cottages appear ahead of me, the moonlight illuminating their outline.

I hear the door to the left most cabin open, the vague shape of a man appearing in the doorway.

"Zane." I call out. "It's Dimitri Ivanov."

"What the fuck is going on?" he calls back, sounding anything but happy for the interruption.

I sigh, stopping. Zane is a fierce fighter, and a man intent upon protecting his woman. He should not be underestimated. "Betrayal and war," I answer, tiredness creeping into my voice.

A light turns on in the cabin, backlighting him, a woman appearing in the window.

"Cadence," he rumbles. "I told you not to—"

"Cadence," Ava cries from my arms. "Cadence!"

With a force I never imagined possible, Cadence shoves Zane to the side, sprints down the steps, and runs toward us. "Ava!"

Ava drops from my arms, landing on her feet before she surges forward, nearly falling. "Cadence." It comes out as a half sob as she stumbles toward her friend.

Zane starts after Cadence, and I fall in step behind Ava until the two women meet each other, wrapping their arms in a tangled embrace that is punctuated with blubbering words I can't understand.

Zane meets my eye, looking completely bewildered. "What the..."

Did he not understand what Ava actually meant to Cadence? I've been crystal clear on the depths Ava would go to help her friend. They are bonded in war, and while complicated, it's a bond that is nearly impossible to break.

Knowing that Ava is capable of that kind of love is part of what makes her perfect for me.

"They've been in the trenches together," I answer Zane's partial question, before I touch Ava's shoulder. "I want you inside, sweetheart. It's safer."

I see her nod, even as Cadence's eyes jump up to mine, her gaze taking in every detail.

I'm watching her right back.

I know she and Ava are opposites in action, but they're also opposites in appearance. Ava is petite but curvy, with blonde hair and blue eyes.

Cadence is tall and lean, built like a model with long, red hair and deep brown eyes that pierce into mine.

While her features are very attractive, there is a hardness in every line that makes her look like a warrior.

Ava pulls back, her arms still around Cadence. "Dimitri's right. Let's go inside."

Cadence is still assessing me. "This is the guy you're dating?"

"That's right."

"Did he get you into this mess?" Cadence's lip curls.

My own features harden. "Are you certain that wasn't you?"

Her eyes narrow. "How dare—"

"Enough," Ava breaks in. While the word brokers no argument, the tone is soft, easy. "I chose to stay by Dimitri's side, Cadence."

Cadence's gaze flicks to Ava and I watch her soften. "We've really got to talk about that, Ava. It's not healthy, how you pick people who lead you into trouble."

Cadence grimaces at her own words and I realize she isn't talking about me, but herself. My shoulders unwind a bit, because I think we've understood each other.

But they stiffen again, when I realize she's right. I have brought heaps of trouble to Ava's door.

Ava releases Cadence with one arm, reaching a hand back to me. "We both know that if left to my own devices, all I would do all the time is work and worry."

Cadence lets out a soft laugh. "Very true. But you could pick people who are run-of-the-mill dangerous. You know, someone who participates in petty theft because they're bored, not because they have anger and abandonment issues."

Zane's hand comes to Cadence's back. "We're working on those." That's when I notice that Zane has a number of bruises all over his arms and face. Has he been having a tough time taming Cadence?

Tazz must notice too, because he clears his throat. "Cadence, is it?"

Zane brushes past Cadence and Ava, blocking them and standing at my shoulder. "Who is this fuck-face?"

A half grin pulls at my lips. "Another contestant and here to help. Now, let's go inside where I can fill you all in on the details."

Zane glares at Tazz. "Fine. But he stays outside." He points at Tazz, before his eyes sweep across the other assembled men. "And these fuckers too."

I shake my head. "The rest of them are happily married, and we all need to understand what's coming. Everyone is coming inside."

Zane's lip curls. "Fine."

"Center house," I call out. "We need a plan and a careful inventory of the weapons at our disposal."

Ava lets go of Cadence to spin back toward me.

Wrapping my arm around her, I tuck her into my side, my lips dropping to her ear. "There isn't anything I wouldn't do to protect you, milaya. Have faith in that."

# CHAPTER TWENTY-FIVE

Ava

I walk into the small house and note, even in the dark, that it smells expensive. Like wool carpet and new appliances.

"We're keeping the lights off," Dimitri quietly states. He's not talking just to me, but to everyone. "Let's not make it too easy to be found."

I wrap my arms about his waist, laying my head on his chest. His arm tightens around my back as he draws me closer.

Tazz steps to my other side and I actually feel safer with him there. It's like the more I'm around men, the less afraid I become.

I wish I'd realized that years ago. That surrounding myself with the right men would help me heal.

Cadence stands next to Zane, his hand on her shoulder, his body slightly in front of hers in a clearly protective stance, though she doesn't need it.

Men have always flocked to Cadence. But if she makes it hard for me to take care of her, with men...she has always been staunchly independent. Aggressively so.

Dimitri begins to speak, sharing information I already know. His father is the head of his family and their business. He's been holding his sisters hostage. He also shares his attempts to force his father's hand. "This is my fight. Any and all of you are welcome to leave. But I ask that you do so now, if you're going to go."

No one moves.

I don't open my eyes to see their faces. I keep them closed, my nose buried in Dimitri's chest. Only my ears are open.

But no one shifts or speaks, the silence is resolute.

I give Dimitri the smallest squeeze.

"He knows Trent brought Ava here, so he'll know I'm here too."

"What's his end game?" Tazz asks.

"Kill me or punish me for trying to gain my independence," Dimitri answers with a slow exhale. "And if it's the latter, then he'll have an eye on forcing me back into the fold."

I squeeze him tighter, my hands spreading out on his back. He continues to hold me close.

"Will he physically attack?" Gris asks.

Dimitri pauses. "In the past, his moves against me have been more…tactical, in that they are meant to manipulate."

"He's been holding your sisters hostage and then he tried to what… Why have Ava pushed into The Hunt?" Luke asks.

I lift my head to look at him, considering. It's a good question.

"I…" Dimitri's hand fists in my shirt. "To test my commitment to her."

Gris makes a low growl in his throat. "And what you proved today was that—"

"I'd kill for her."

That makes my head snap up, my eyes going wide as I look up at Dimitri's chiseled jaw. "What does that mean?" I ask, my voice barely above a whisper.

But his other arm is around me as he lifts me off the ground. "Gris. I need you to get Ava out of here. I've made a mistake—"

A red dot appears on the wall behind us.

"Everyone down," Tazz barks out, pushing Dimitri with me in his arms. We crash to the ground, Dimitri twisting so that he lands hard on his shoulder, protecting my body from the fall.

A second later, shots ring out, a high-powered rifle littering the walls and ceiling with bullets. I don't even have time to register the fear, as Dimitri covers me, protecting my body with his.

It goes on and on, lasting for what feels like forever. My hands cover my ears as I shrink deeper into his protection.

He rolls on top of me, his hands coming to my ears too.

I sob into his shirt, squeezing him until my entire body aches.

The noise stops as suddenly as it started. I only have one second to relax into the silence before the tension of not knowing what will happen next hits full force.

"Dimitri," a man's deep and familiar baritone calls from outside. It lacks Dimitri's honey, but I know it's his father without being told.

"Otets," Dimitri replies. "To what do we owe this pleasure?" He doesn't get up. If anything, his grip around me tightens.

"You know very well." I practically hear the sneer in his heavily accented voice.

"I'm not sure I do," Dimitri answers as he slowly releases me. He sits up, but as I go to follow, he holds his hand out to stop me.

"You're selling a lot of real estate, son."

"Not yours. Only mine." Dimitri's hand splays out on my belly, before he looks over at Gris who is slowly sitting up.

Gris nods and then crawls over to us. Dimitri stands as Gris blocks my body.

"You know very well that you made the money to buy them from my business."

"No. My business. My payment for running your casino," Dimitri rolls his shoulders out.

"Everything in this family is mine, Dimitri. You know that very well."

"I do." Dimitri takes a step forward, toward the doorway. "Shall we discuss terms?"

"What makes you think there are terms?" is his father's reply.

"I assume, if you don't want me to continue with the sale of the three properties, you're here to offer an alternative?"

"No alternative. Don't sell them or you'll never see your sisters again. Have I not been clear?"

I see Dimitri draw taller, my own heart hammering in my chest. "You've been clear. Which is how I know you're not allowing me to see them either way."

There is a pause, the thickness of it making it hard to breathe. "You think you are going to force my hand?" I can hear the razor-sharp edge in his father's words, the danger in them, making me shiver.

And then the cock of a gun fills the silence, my own body jerking in response.

A feral snarl rips from Dimitri's lips, but I can't see what's happening. "Don't."

# CHAPTER TWENTY-SIX

DIMITRI

I OPEN the door that barely hangs off its hinges

My father stands with Sasha and Katarina to his right, both of them hunched down and holding each other.

Several men flank him on either side, one with the automatic rifle in his hand. He'll pay for what he's done. After.

Because right now, my father has a pistol aimed at Sasha's temple. He cocks the hammer, the click jolting through me.

"Don't," I snarl, every muscle in my body turning to stone. I know I'm challenging my father like never before. That I'm drawing this confrontation to a head, but I have to remember…he's never fought fair, and he won't today.

"I only need one of your sisters to make the trade with the Smiths. I only need to give up one casino. You'll do as I say, boy, or it's her life." He's making it clear. This isn't a negotiation. I am to sell one casino and only one. And in exchange, Sasha keeps her life. That's it.

I raise my hands in the air. I need to break from my father to keep

Ava and Anna safe. But I can't do it in exchange for Sasha's life. I'd never be able to forgive myself. "I'm sure there's another way."

He lowers the gun, eyeing me with a gleam that fills me with dread. "Let me think..."

The hair on the back of my neck stands up.

I'm not afraid of my father. I'm not afraid of death either.

But the damage he can inflict on the people I love, that frightens me more than anything in the world.

"Otets," I growl out low, knowing he doesn't deserve the title of father.

"I'd consider a trade."

Fuck. I already know what he's going to say and my fingers ball into fists. "No."

"Give me Ava and I'll let you have Sasha and Katarina." An evil smile curls his lips.

Gris was right. He used Trent to test Ava's importance in my life and now that he knows, he's found an even better tool to control me. The woman I love.

He raises the gun again, back to Sasha's temple. "I'll shoot her Dimitri. You'd better decide and be quick."

I open my mouth to drop every obscenity under the sun when a soft hand brushes my back. "I agree to the terms."

My head whips around, even as Ava steps past me. "The fuck you do." I reach out my hand, wrapping my fingers around her upper arm.

She gives me this smile, soft, sweet, full of love and the slightest bit of apology. "Let me help you."

"No fucking way," Cadence spits from behind me. Honestly, she took the words right out of my mouth. "Ava Tantor, don't you even think about sacrificing yourself. You can love someone without killing yourself."

But Ava doesn't answer as she pulls out of my grip like she's just going to walk up to my father. Like he's not going to take all three of them and disappear, trapping me so tightly I can't breathe.

She doesn't understand this will never be fair.

I reach out to grab her arm again, to stop her, when a shuffle happens behind me. My head snaps around in time to see Cadence with a gun in her hand.

My mouth opens to shout my objection as she fires. I hear the shot, feel it move the air. One second and then two passes before my father stumbles back.

And then the world explodes.

# CHAPTER TWENTY-SEVEN

Ava

Everything happens at once.

I'm under Dimitri before I can even scream, the bullet having passed so close to me, I think it singed my hair.

"My sisters," Dimitri yells, and the men around us burst into action. But he doesn't move. His arms wrap around me, enveloping me in a cocoon. "Don't you ever do that again."

He sounds angry. He's never spoken to me with a tone like that before, but I know it's just the fear talking. So, I wrap my arms around his neck. "I love you too."

He chokes squeezing me tight.

"Dimitri," I whisper. "Go get your sisters. Cadence will keep me safe."

He lifts his head, looking down at me with dark and stormy eyes. "I keep you safe. Always."

"Go," I say back. "Once you have them, we'll all be safe."

He lifts off me, Cadence standing just to our right with the gun in her hand. Zane rips it from her fingers. "I'll keep them both safe."

Dimitri nods and then he's out the door. The moment he's gone, Zane spits at Cadence. "What the fuck were you thinking?"

I open my mouth to answer, assuming he's talking about my move to hand myself over, but it's Cadence who puffs out her chest, her chin lifting. "I'll keep them both safe?" She spits back. "I want to be clear about something. I can let go of unnecessary violence, but I'm not turning into some helpless female." She steps up, to Zane, tilting her chin to glare in his eyes. She's tall but he's way taller, his tattooed biceps rippling as he clenches a fist. "I already told you. Saving my best friend doesn't count as unnecessary violence."

"You shot a man!" Zane throws his hands in the air.

I'm still lying on the floor. I pull myself up very slowly, not wanting to interrupt.

"To be fair, I only hit his arm." Cadence shrugs. "That's progress for me."

Zane reaches a hand down to me, pulling me up to my feet before he's ushering us both behind the kitchen island where we've got some small bit of protection and we're hidden from view.

Once we're behind the cabinet, he rumbles, "How is this progress?"

I shift my attention back to the action outside, realizing the two of them are having nothing more than a squabble. I peek around the cabinet trying to catch a glimpse of Dimitri. Is he all right?

Cadence scoffs next to me. "The last man who attacked Cadence, I stabbed in the throat with an ice pick."

That turns my head back to my friend and her man. "I'm still really grateful for that."

"You're grateful she stabbed a man?" Zane gives me the sort of hard look that makes me shrink.

Cadence leans forward, cutting of Zane's view of me and putting herself between us. "Don't look at her like that."

"Like what?" Zane asks, sounding confused.

I draw in a deep breath. "I was being raped by our foster father." It's getting easier to say the words. They really did need to be let out and the more I do, the more I feel the fear receding.

Zane makes a noise that I don't understand. "That's why you stabbed him?" His voice is quiet. "Is that why you have the dreams?"

"I know I need to work on the anger," Cadence's voice has calmed. "But sometimes..."

"You're the warrior," he answers. "I know, sweetheart. But it eats you too. You need to let someone else fight sometimes so that you can have some peace."

She nods, and I reach for her hand, lacing my fingers through hers. "I'm sorry if I set your progress back. I'll leave you alone to—"

"Don't you dare," she leans into me. "Every time I leave you, I remember why I need you. I'm sorry that I keep disappearing. That's my shit, not yours."

"Cade," I breathe, my throat catching as it closes. "I love you forever. There isn't anything I wouldn't do to help you be your best."

Slowly, Zane lowers his hand over the tops of ours. "I think I'm starting to understand."

"Ava," Dimitri calls from the door. "Milaya."

I stick my head out from behind the cabinet, my eyes catching his. "Dimitri."

His two sisters stand on either side of him as I let go of Cadence and scramble to rise and launch myself into his arms. "You did it."

He catches me to his chest, dropping his face into the crook of my neck. "I did not."

I lean back, my eyes going wide as they meet his.

# CHAPTER TWENTY-EIGHT

DIMITRI

I HOLD Ava in my arms, equal parts relieved and afraid.

I've got my sisters. My woman.

It's almost everything I hoped for.

But my father has escaped. I have no idea how wounded he is, there is blood but until the light of day, I won't be able to tell how much.

His men closed around him, leaving my sisters as they made their escape.

Tazz was shot, and Gris nearly so, but that's the total of our damage.

All in all, it's a win, but I wanted to end this. I take solace in the fact that he can't hurt any of the women I love, but that doesn't mean he won't try again.

I've won a battle but not the war and the next time we fight, there will be nothing holding either of us back.

"What do you mean you didn't do it?" Ava asks, her eyes wide with her fear.

"He means," Sasha scoffs, "that our father still lives. Unfortunately." Her disdain is completely evident. Who can blame her? He just held a gun to her head.

Sasha has always been…special. Intelligent beyond belief, she lacks a certain filter that other people inherently have. I agree with her, of course. But perhaps everyone doesn't need to know we want our father dead. Then again, if ever a crowd of people would understand, it's this one.

"We're still in danger?" Ava asks.

Katarina looks over at me and asks me in Russian, "You couldn't have chosen a Russian woman? She'd be able to fight, not just hang on your neck like a child."

I grimace, but don't answer. I don't need to explain to my sister the choice of my heart. "You're welcome," I say in English. "I've thought of little besides your safety."

Katarina narrows her eyes at me. These past five years of being trapped with my father have hardened both my sisters, and I hurt for them. What they've lost will be nearly impossible to replace.

Gris steps in next to me, his sleeve singed from the bullet that almost landed in his arm. "We should find somewhere hidden and secure to take all of you until we know your father isn't in the city any longer."

I nod, taking one hand from around Ava to clap Gris on the shoulder. "Thank you, brother." It's my way of telling him I know what he's done for me. For us. And that we are bonded now.

Gris gives me a single nod. He understands.

His phone rings and looking at the screen, he picks up, speaking quietly. When he's done, he waves me toward him. I set Ava down, reluctantly, as I take a step toward him. "It was Killian."

"Yes?" My heart begins to race in my chest.

"There was an attack at your apartment."

My chest grows so tight, I can't even push out words.

"He wants to know what he should do with the bodies."

"Which…"

Gris eyes me, his voice dropping, "He killed them before they even entered the building."

Relief makes me limp. But Triston was right before. My home isn't safe. I turn to Gris. "Have you got somewhere in mind we can go?"

Tazz enters the small space too, making it beyond crowded. "I'm going to need rubbing alcohol and some bandages."

"You were shot," Gris scoffs, watching the blood drip down Tazz's thigh.

"Right. That's why I need the alcohol." He pushes past me toward the bathroom. I watch him disappear with a shake of my head. He's as tough as any Russian. I might just hire him.

Gris watches him too. "If I get shot, I'm going to need more than rubbing alcohol."

"I'll make sure you've got whisky," I answer with a small wink. I like Gris. While Triston is the head of the family and often prickly, Gris has an ease about him. It's why he's in charge of public relations.

He smiles back. "In terms of where we tuck you and your family away, the Kincaids keep a few buildings empty and under shell companies for just these kinds of situations."

Noted. It's a move I'll make in the future, to have secret holdings for hiding out when necessary.

For now, I start shuttling everyone from the house out to the cars. Every able-bodied man sets a perimeter, though it's an unnecessary precaution as no one attacks.

We load into the cars and speed off toward Vegas.

Tomorrow, we'll have to clean up this whole mess. Tonight, though, is about keeping everyone safe.

It feels like it takes all night, but Anna is collected, bags are packed, and we're moved in small batches to a state-of-the-art, empty, apartment building.

Several of the Kincaids are there, along with most of the Smith family.

Ryker Smith stands in the line of Smith brothers, his dark eyes assessing both of my sisters.

He looks more like Killian with rougher, harsher features, rather than the smooth good looks of Triston and Gris, but I hear one of my sister's gasps, nonetheless. I turn to them, wondering which it might have been, but both have pulled their features into expressionless masks. Who reacted? Was it fear?

Or did one of them realize he's the man who's been promised to Katarina?

I can't attend the puzzle now, as we're moved into several apartments. The building, I've been told, was built like a bomb shelter.

My sisters are in one, Anna, Ava, and I in another, and Gertrude into a small unit at the end of the hall.

Despite being dragged to this place in the middle of the night, she gasps when she sees the place and promptly offers, "I'll stay as long as you need, Mr. Ivanov."

I nod my agreement. Under the circumstances, it suits all of us best that Gertrude stays for as long as possible.

In addition, Ryker and Rush Smith plan to stay on the floor below us, and tomorrow, Killian and his wife will join them to help create a bubble of protection.

"Ava and Chloe have a lot in common," Triston assures me. I'm not surprised. Killian instantly understood Ava's problems and he had ready answers to put her at ease.

I shake my head. The hitman that is an advocate for abused women. It has...a certain poetry.

Much like my own situation, I suppose.

Ava takes Anna to put her to bed, and I meet with Jake Kincaid, head of their security, and now mine.

Jake leads me to a small room on the first floor of the building where three men sit with twenty screens in front of them. "I have workers who will watch the cameras twenty-four hours a day, seven days a week. I've added your number to the alert list. But in the case of most emergencies, you should just stay put. The Vendettis bombed this building and it didn't move. In addition, I've turned the elevators into vaults. If we stop them, no one is getting in or out."

I give a curt nod. "And the stairwells?"

He hands me a key card. "Reinforced steel, a bullet can't puncture them, and a bomb won't touch them. Locked tight."

"Why don't you and your family just live here?"

Jake gives a humorless chuckle, shaking his head. "We tried. Nearly killed each other. It turns out, we need a bit of space. Family that works together is hard enough. Living together too..." He leans closer. "Mason and Leo dented up one of the elevators so badly, I had to replace it. It's when I came up with the idea to up the security in them."

"I see. Thank you," I respond with a nod.

"We keep the building for emergencies though, and you are welcome to stay for as long as you like."

I'm not sure how I'm going to repay the Smiths and the Kincaids, but I know I'll spend a lifetime trying.

By the time I make it back upstairs, Anna is sound asleep. I watch her for a moment, before I begin searching for Ava.

I find her curled under the covers of the king-sized bed, naked, her hair still damp from her shower.

I step into the bathroom, rinsing myself off too. Then, naked, I crawl into bed next to her.

She wakes as soon as my weight depresses the mattress and I've barely laid down, when she presses into my side. "You're here."

"I never left, milaya," I murmur into her temple as I wrap my arms around her, pulling her on top of me.

"I know, but you weren't in bed with me, and I just worried you'd decided this was all too much..." she tapers off, her lips finding mine.

The kiss is achingly sweet, and her mouth just makes me desperate for more. But I have this moment where I understand...this whole time, she's been afraid I might reject her.

That I wouldn't be willing to accept her fears, her limitations.

But it's my past, my shit, that almost destroyed us both tonight.

"Ava," I say against her mouth.

She picks up her head. Looking down at me. "What's wrong?"

My jaw hardens as my hands splay out on her back. "You were nearly destroyed tonight and that was before you were nearly killed."

She looks down at me in confusion. "But you saved me."

"Maybe." I look away then, pain pulling my mouth down into a frown.

"What do you mean, maybe...."

"Ava," my throat fills with pain. "I'm the reason all that trouble happened. Without me—"

"Without you, I'd still be locked inside a prison of my own making."

I look back at her, knowing that I should argue. "Men tried to hunt you tonight."

"That did suck," she nods, her elbows coming to my chest as she props herself up. "But it was also a bit like facing my worst fear and living through it. I'm not seventeen anymore. I'm a grown woman who can rewire her neural pathways or whatever. And..."

She stops to draw in a deep breath, and I take that opportunity to shake my head. "Who told you about neural pathways?" I demand, my college studies feeling like some distant life. But before she can answer, I push the question aside. It doesn't matter. "I'm at the beginning of a war, Ava. I hoped to end it tonight, but I should have known...it's just beginning."

"You're going to need me, then," she says simply.

I choke on the emotion that rises in my chest. "I don't want to see you hurt, sweetheart."

"What happens if something happens to you? I'm an orphan, Dimitri. Anna needs to be protected, at the very least, I can help you with that."

I stare at her at a complete loss for words. This woman...

# CHAPTER TWENTY-NINE

AVA

I HEAR everything Dimitri is saying, and I think I might even understand where he's coming from.

But the color he's brought to my life is now a rainbow I can't live without. And loving someone is about loving all of them, the good with the bad.

That's always been something I can do.

He's not shaking me. I love Anna and I love him. I'm here for the long haul.

"Ava," he pushes out, his normally honey voice sounding...broken.

It eats at me, that tone. Maybe I've got it wrong. Maybe tonight made him think that I'm not right for him. Maybe he's decided he doesn't want me.

My chin droops into my hand. If he doesn't want me...

My life really would lose the color again, the idea of losing him twists in my side like a sharp knife. But also, I'd know that I was capable of seeing it, feeling it, and I'd be better for it. That doesn't make me want him less. "Don't say my name like that."

"Like what?"

"Like it hurts you," I whisper and then I start to roll away.

But he holds me firm. "It did hurt me to hurt you tonight. That's my whole point."

"Is it? Or is your point that you've decided you don't want me?" I pull away then, rolling off him and onto my back.

But he rolls with me, his body hovering above mine in a plank position. "Dimitri."

"Am I frightening you, love?"

It's the love that makes me relax. The single word is full of so much concern that I reach my arms around his neck, putting pressure on his neck to make him lower himself. "No. I want your skin on mine."

Slowly, gently, he lowers himself. "You're sure?"

In response, I wrap my legs around his hips, pulling his body into the cradle of mine. "You don't scare me, Dimitri. If anything…"

"What?"

"I feel safe with your body over mine. I'm home in your arms." I look into his eyes, willing him to see the truth.

He must, because he leans down, his mouth covering mine, kissing me long and slow. "I'd never want to hurt you, milaya, but also, it's my job to protect you and that might mean not being at my side. You're safer away from me."

I relax into the mattress, the tip of his cock nestling against my folds. "I'm meant to be at your side. Always." I meant what I said about Anna. "Unless you need me to take Anna away. That's different."

He sinks inside me, holding my gaze. "You'd do that for me? For my daughter?"

"I'd do anything for you and for her. You're my family," I answer as he bottoms out inside me.

"I love you, Ava. You are my heart." He devours my mouth even as he pulls out only to sink back in.

My whole body sings along with his, so I don't answer until his mouth finally lifts. "I love you too."

"Tell me you'll be my wife. That you'll marry me." He pushes back inside me, the thrust so good, I'm arching off the bed.

"Yes," I gasp, hanging onto his neck, my chin pushing up to leave my neck exposed to him.

He kisses along the column, picking up the pace, his thrusts pushing me closer and closer to orgasm.

The feel of his skin above me, his strength, only makes me hotter, and I dig my fingers into the thick muscles of his back, holding him tightly.

He starts to roll over again, to pull me back on top, but I tighten my thighs on his hips. "Are you sure?" he asks me, holding my face in his hands.

"I'm sure," I answer, kissing him again, twining my tongue with his.

If I could think, I'd marvel at the way masculinity has been rewritten for me. It's the strength that he uses for me, for my benefit, rather than against, that has changed.

Dimitri's body brings me protection, pleasure, love. I arch deeper, my back bowing as I take more of him, the hum of the impending orgasm making me taut as a bow string.

"Dimitri," I gasp out, digging my nails into his skin.

"That's it, my love, let me fill you."

"Yes," I moan back, meeting each of his thrusts as I tilt my hips to take more of him. "You feel so good like this." To be fair, he feels good in every position, and I can't wait to try lots more.

"So do you," he rumbles into my neck. "I'll never get enough of you, Ava. You were made for me."

I can't answer, I'm too far gone, my entire body focused on the pleasure that's building inside. But if I could, I'd tell him that he was made for me too. Since the first moment I met him, I sensed what I refused to acknowledge, this man was my home.

"Cum for me. Cum all over me," he growls into my ear. "Let me fill you."

I cry out, my legs locked around him as I seek more friction, more pleasure and then I break, a scream pulling from my lips.

My orgasm triggers his and he starts to cum, his body shaking and twitching as his muscles push his seed deep inside me.

I hold him close, my arms and legs holding him tight as he collapses on top of me so that I'm completely tucked underneath him.

There isn't a bit of fear with his body on mine, only contentment, as I drift off to sleep.

# EPILOGUE

DIMITRI

*TWO WEEKS LATER...*

TODAY IS MY WEDDING DAY.

It's odd. I've been here before. Well not here, exactly.

But I've been married. My first wedding was a lavish affair, a fabricated romance, meant to fool the world. But this wedding is simple. Small.

And filled with so much love, I think I might burst from it.

We're in our borrowed apartment. We could go back to my home —my father hasn't been seen anywhere in Las Vegas since that night in the woods.

But I like the security of being here, my family is safer surrounded by security and in a building meant to survive the war of the worlds.

Ava has been able to work remotely, though she'll have to go back into the office soon. I've already discussed transportation for her, and it includes a driver, and a specialty car designed to be bulletproof. The Kincaids have one already and are having another fabricated for our use.

I'd ask her not to go to work, but I know the woman I'm marrying. Quitting her profession isn't an option.

A small crowd stands in the kitchen. Several Kincaids, Smiths, and my sisters, of course, along with a few of the men in my operation I consider friends.

In the back stands Zane, because Cadence is helping Ava prepare.

Standing in front of me is Killian Smith, the man who we chose to officiate the ceremony.

No one is as shocked as me, but I think that Killian might have become my most trusted friend. The shadow has a heart that's made of gold.

"After the ceremony, we need to talk," he murmurs as the violinist takes her seat.

"About?"

"New identities for Ava and Anna."

My head whips around, the crowd forgotten. "What?"

"I have one for Chloe," he waves at his wife, and she waves back. "If anything happens to me, she has offshore accounts, a home bought by a shell company, and a new identity. She can disappear. We should do the same for your family."

My jaw works as I try to find the words. Killian continues to prove why he's become a trusted friend. "You're right. Thank you."

He nods. "My pleasure. I don't say this about many women, but your Ava is one of the good ones. You know that I'll do whatever I can to help."

I have to look away, I'm so overwhelmed. "From you, that promise is worth more than gold." Because while my father has gone underground. He is coming back.

And there will be a war.

I look at my two sisters. Keeping them safe is next on my to-do list.

But that is forgotten for the moment.

Because the violinist begins to play and my bride appears. She wears a simple gown of pale blue, so light, it's nearly white.

I know she picked the color because she didn't quite feel right about wearing true white. I let her make the decision.

But to me, she is one of the most beautifully pure people I've ever met, and I'll spend my life protecting all the good I see shining out from the inside of her soul.

I reach out my hand, resisting the urge to race down the aisle and collect her into my arms.

My soon-to-be wife.

The love of my life.

Behind her, Anna appears. She wears a toddler gown in the same fabric and color as Ava's, flowers crowning her head. In her hand, the gift I gave her this morning: a new mama doll for her dollhouse with blonde hair.

She jumps, making the flowing skirts flounce out. "I pretty!"

The crowd gives a small laugh as Ava bends down and kisses Anna's cheek. "You're beautiful."

I can't stand it anymore. "Come, my loves." And then I start for them. Because while patience is a virtue of mine, so is commitment.

And I don't want to wait another second to make us a family for real.

Dear Readers,

Thank you to all of you who have been reading along with my *"Kings of Las Vegas"* series! As I wrote Dimitri and Ava's story, I knew that Cadence and Zane's story needed to be told too. It's too good to leave behind!

Please keep reading for the surprise second story, The King of the Hunt!

. . .

All my best,
Tammy

# KING OF THE HUNT

TAMMY ANDRESEN

**I just agreed to enter The Hunt...**

I need a change.
A chance to break old patterns…
But maybe agreeing to be hunted wasn't the best choice for making that happen.

*Then again, 'bad choice' should be my middle name....*

# CHAPTER ONE

Cadence

"Players, set..." A speaker, from somewhere in the trees, crackles.

I look up into the canopy but can't identify where the noise is coming from in the dark.

To my right, I hear the soft rustle of grass and crouch down, holding in my intake of breath. What was that? Who?

Fear tightens my limbs as I cock my head, listening to the darkness.

In the distance I hear masculine voices, grunting, calling out in barely contained aggression as they stomp their feet. I spread my hands out on the cool, damp ground as I take a long, slow breath of air.

The players must be on the other side of the field from me. It's good to know I have that kind of head start, but I swear I feel the ground shake from their excitement.

This was a bad idea.

Which should not surprise me. I'm full of them. In fact, I'd say it's the story of my life. Cadence Bad Idea Miller. That ought to be my name.

I tremble, sinking down lower to the ground. Is now the time to run? Hide?

The organizers assured me this was perfectly safe, but it doesn't feel safe at all. In fact, it feels like...

My worst nightmare come to life.

My fingers curl into the dirt. Maybe that's what I need. To face the fear that has eaten at me my entire adult life so that I can move past it and be...

Normal?

The thought makes my lips curl, and I straighten back up. Who wants to be normal? Boring.

I scrub a hand over my cheeks, pushing the thoughts away. This exact tug of war is what gets me in trouble every time. Part of me craves a quieter life and the other, seeks conflict and chaos.

I can't sit still ever. Can't stay in a job or a place. And forget about a relationship. Most times a guy pisses me off, and then I blow the whole thing up.

Most of the time I create the explosion with words. A few times, it's gotten physical.

But growing up in foster care isn't exactly the place to learn about balanced, kind reactions when dealing with other people. There is little that's normal, or stable, in that environment. It's the jungle.

And you either learn to fight or die.

And before foster care, I lived with my crackhead mother—talk about instability. The shit I saw by the time I was six...

That thought makes me stand straight and tall. I'm a girl who knows how to fight. And that is what I do today. I fight.

If one of those jackasses on the other side of the field thinks I'm just going to submit to him, he's got another thing coming. If he wants me, he's going to have to work for it.

I give myself a shake. The organizer of this event told me that The Hunt was a way for me to rewrite my brain to respond differently to danger. To not react so violently, so emotionally.

But now that I'm here, I'm thinking, fuck that. I'm going to fight. My chaos goblin wants out.

I toss back my shoulders, getting ready, as a horn blast fills the air, the shrill sound so loud, for a moment I drop into a crouch again, holding my ears.

The sound slowly dies, echoing over the open air, replaced by the thunderous beat of men's feet.

Despite my commitment to bravery, I shrink again, at least for a second. I'm tall for a woman, just over five feet eight inches, so cowering doesn't help all that much.

Gathering myself up, I push my shock of red hair over my shoulder and move into the line of trees, jumping up to grab a branch and then swing myself up on the limb.

One of the high schools I attended had a rope-course adventure unit. It was one of the best times I had in school and I use the skills I learned now, settling into a crouch on the branch as the thundering footfalls of the men grow closer.

The man who agreed to let me compete, Dimitri Ivanov, told me some women fight, and some women hide, but all end up giving themselves to their chosen fighter. His words give me a one-second pause.

Am I going to surrender to a man? Try and set aside my past, ignore the restless energy inside me, and let a man claim me?

I doubt it.

Which is why, when a fighter veers toward my tree, my muscles tense, readying for the fight.

For a moment, I think he's spotted me, but then he passes under my branch. I could stay hidden. Wait for one of them to find me, but that isn't my style.

So, grabbing the branch again, I swing down, my feet slamming into his back as I push with all the weight and muscle I have. He lurches forward, flying through the air and lands on his stomach.

"Ha," I shout into the night, adrenaline rushing through me. Fighting makes me feel powerful, in control, in a world where women are so often victims. Where I am a victim.

But either his fall or my gloating catches the notice of another man. Tall and broad, I no longer have the element of surprise.

And while I'm tall, I'm also slender, and no match for this guy in a one-to-one confrontation.

Unless...

I stand perfectly still, his advance making my muscles twitch with the effort not to move.

At the last possible second, when his massive hands are almost on me, I drop, punching out and hitting him square in the groin.

He drops like a stone, his cry of pain echoing through the field, but I don't hesitate. Instead, I break out into a run, racing toward the field that the hunters have just exited.

But I haven't made it more than two yards when fingers lock around my biceps in an iron grip.

I scream, a reflex I can't control as the man yanks hard. I hit his chest, my jaw snapping shut, and I bite my own tongue, a cry of pain rushing through my lips.

But it doesn't even slow him as he drops me to the ground, blood filling my mouth. He grabs the waist of my athletic leggings and rips them down my body.

I scream, paralyzing fear knocking the fight out of me. This was not part of the deal. I lash out with a hand, but before I can land the hit, he traps it in his, which is easily twice the size of mine.

I try again with my other hand, but he grabs that one too, pushing it up above my head with the other, like I'm not offering any resistance at all, and then locks both my wrists in his one hand.

Using his one free hand, he tears the leggings and then he starts to pull his pants down his hips, working his thighs between mine. "No," I cry out, but my legs offer so little resistance.

This can't be how it's supposed to go. That I am forced to live out my worst nightmare. "Stop." But the blood in my mouth gurgles my words. "Please stop."

The please comes out jagged and raw, a word I don't utter very often.

"Shut up," he spits, grabbing my panties even as I gasp out a sob. He rips again, my underwear breaking like they're made of paper.

I cry out and he raises his hand to smack my face. It comes down hard across my cheek, pain exploding through my skull. Blood sprays out of my mouth, misting his face. He doesn't notice.

I squeeze my eyes shut, preparing for the invasion that's about to come. I have this fleeting thought about my best friend, Ava.

I watched her be raped, a memory I dream often. Sometimes I'm me, stabbing her attacker in the neck, and sometimes…I'm her.

But the dreams didn't prepare me for how this would actually feel. "Ava," I whimper, knowing I've never fully understood her pain.

For how it would feel to be trapped like this, under a man who is immune to my suffering. I ache for me, but honestly, I ache for her. I haven't given her enough grace. Enough love.

My thoughts are slammed back to the present as he bends down, his teeth sinking into my neck like some sick fucking animal. He's about to break the flesh when from out of nowhere….

I hear the thud of flesh hitting flesh and suddenly I'm free. I sit up to see the man who'd just held me down laying in the dirt. Standing next to me, another fighter. I start to scurry away in a crab crawl, despite being naked from the waist down, when he bends down and catches my ankle.

I panic, kicking out, but his grip doesn't tighten. His hand isn't rough, just firm as he says in a quiet voice, "Settle, sweetheart."

I blink back my surprise, the fear still tensing my limbs, as I note the rippling muscles on display in his tank top. He has on army-style pants, his hair cropped short. Soldier? "Are you going to try and rape me too?"

But I can already feel the difference. We're talking, his eyes are calm, his touch deliberate, but not hostile.

Good God, he's handsome. Not pretty at all, his features are rough and masculine, but they're still nicely arrayed.

His eyes flick to the other man lying in the grass, growing diamond-hard before they return to mine, and then soften. "No, sweetheart. You're safe with me."

"Safe?" I ask, and my voice catches again. I swallow down my fear. There is no place for it here. "You're not trying to..." I was going to say, get in my pants, but I don't have any currently.

"We're going to have sex. And we're *both* going to love it. Promise."

# CHAPTER TWO

CADENCE

FOR A SECOND, I just stare at him. Is he crazy? After what just happened, no one is touching me.

And then I remember. The Hunt ends when I let one of them have me.

*Let* being the operative word and the one the last man had clearly forgotten. But until then, the hunters will keep coming...

And any one of the men I've run into already might take another go. Whatever their reason for entering this competition, they all want to win.

And the prize is fucking me.

I signed up for this...

The soldier pulls me close enough to hook his other arm around my waist. His movements are slow and careful, despite the danger that surrounds us.

Which is why, I don't resist as he lifts me into his arms, straightening up while holding me so we're both standing. "Decision?"

I appreciate that he's asking my permission. This isn't a moment to be weak, it will only make the whole situation worse and bravery is one of the few attributes I've got in spades.

"Yes," I answer simply, making my choice.

Maybe it's his gentleness that allows me to give in to him. He isn't like the others. Which is why I'm choosing him.

Not that he's weak. My soldier boy just knocked a man out. A really strong one, at that.

I'm not wearing leggings or underwear, so he only has to yank at the waist of his cargo pants, the heavy fabric dropping to his knees.

I look down to see the kind of cock I've only ever dreamed about. He's not even fully erect and he's so thick that it makes my mouth water. Or maybe that's the blood from my wounded tongue.

He bends a bit, hooking my knee and wrapping one of my legs around his waist.

And then he plunges inside me.

I should be shocked. Scandalized even.

But as he sinks deeply, every nerve lights on fire and my head tips back, a cry of a completely different kind falling from my lips. He feels so good, I forget everything else.

But once he's inside me, he stops, his body freezing in place as his muscles grow completely rigid against my softer flesh. "Why is there blood on your chin?"

He asks it like he's angry. I blink at him in confusion, too wrapped up in how he feels to process the question.

The PA crackles. "Game over."

My soldier boy pulls out of me, and I make the smallest whimper of regret as I'm left feeling empty without him. He could have kept going. I would have welcomed it.

I dig my fingers into his shoulders, my leg tightening around his waist, my invitation not spoken but still totally obvious.

"In a minute, sweetheart, I'll give you everything you want." His voice is quiet as he tips his forehead down to rest on mine. It's a moment of intimacy that I haven't experienced in a very long time, and it steals my breath.

I stare at him, my lips parting from my surprise and that's when more blood streaks down my chin.

He makes this snarling growl that reverberates in his chest and moves through me. I blink in surprise, wondering at the change and if I've made a terrible mistake.

Did I let the wrong man claim me?

He steps back, his hands raising in a way that makes me cringe, and I hate it. I hate showing fear like that.

The bonded feeling is gone, replaced with anger, as my own fists ball at my sides and I'm ready to fight no matter the outcome.

It's not healthy, but it's me. Aggression brings out aggression in me every time.

But instead of raising his hand to me, he wipes my chin. Then, he shrugs off his tank top, dropping the fabric over my head.

It falls down my thighs, covering the exposed parts of my body. My eyes widen in surprise. Why did he do that for me? He can't care about what other men are seeing, can he? We've known each other for mere minutes. Why is he protecting me in this small way?

I don't have a chance to ask, shirtless, he turns back to the man who caused my tongue to bleed. "Get up, motherfucker," my soldier boy snarls.

The guy sits up, looking dazed, but I still take a step back. I've have taken on many fights that I never should have touched, so it isn't sense that makes me shrink, it's straight-up fear.

No one has ever made me feel as powerless as that piece of shit in the dirt, not since I was a small child. It's a feeling I hate more than any other.

My soldier catches my reaction and his hand brushes down my arm, his fingers gentle before he steps in front of me. "I am going to give you until the count of three to collect yourself and run before I beat you senseless."

"The Hunt is over," the other man spits. "You won."

"It's not about winning," soldier boy fires back. "It's about treating the woman, who gave herself to us, with the respect she deserves."

"Fuck off," the other man barks. "You can go fuck yourself—"

"Three." And then soldier boy dives forward, tackling the other man back to the ground.

I bring both my hands to my mouth to hold in the scream as the two men roll in the dirt, fists flying.

I can't tell who's winning, only that they are both hitting each other with a force that would knock most men out cold.

"Fighting is over," the PA crackles.

Soldier boy wrestles to the top and drops his fist into the other man's face once, twice, three times with a punishing force that reverberates through the ground, the sick sound of it filling the air, before he stands up. "When you're having your dental work done, I want you to remember that gentlemen do not hit ladies. Ever."

And then soldier boy kicks dirt over the other man before he turns back to me.

I raise my brows, my eyes wide with my surprise. I've pictured this kind of moment. One where instead of just blowing up my life, I actually teach another person a lesson about respect.

Mostly, I just get smacked back when I try.

And if I'm honest, no one has ever fought like that for me before. Never.

My bestie, Ava, picks me up when I fall. She's amazing like that. But she's not a fighter. Never has been.

Soldier boy walks back toward me, but his eyes aren't on me, they're behind me. I turn to find three other men standing where the path winds into the forest.

Two are men I knocked down myself, the other stares at me with a raw hunger that makes me shiver.

Behind them, several more men stand in a neat line. They are all in black with their faces covered. A shiver of dread creeps down my spine.

"Guards. They won't hurt us." Soldier boy wraps his arms around my upper legs, lifting me in the air.

"Where were they when that shitbag was attacking me?" I glare at them as I hold onto soldier boy's shoulders.

"They were there," he answers. "They would have intervened if I hadn't." And then he starts walking toward the guards.

My head whips back to him as I suck in a breath. "What are you doing?" I hiss. I'm not the girl who gets carried, and with men all around us, it feels like he should be free to fight.

"Proving a point," he answers, my stomach coming to his chest as I place my hands on his bare shoulders. "You're mine."

His muscles ripple under my hands, the breadth of his shoulders and muscled biceps easily carrying my weight. While part of me would like to argue, his skin against mine makes me feel way safer. But I still hate that he's carrying me closer to a hostile looking group of men. Some of my worst fears have been pricked tonight and I'm completely raw.

"Don't be scared, sweetheart," he murmurs as he walks. "I won't let any of them hurt you."

"I'm not scared," I lie, which is another pattern I like to repeat. When in doubt, bluff.

His arms tighten around my thighs. "I'm glad you're not, but either way, none of them are touching you. You can bet on that."

"You're going to fight all of them off?"

He smiles up at me. "I'd have some help, wouldn't I, little lioness?"

Heat fills my cheeks. "How do you know that?"

"I saw you, from across the field, take out two fighters. Impressive."

I dip my head lower, curling around him as we pass by the very men he's discussing. "Thank you."

"You could have been in the military."

"Maybe." I'm not sure an organization like that would have me, it requires a stability I lack, but I keep that to myself. No need to ruin his idea of me in the first five minutes.

"What's your name?" We enter the woods following a path that I can barely see as he moves with complete ease.

I'm aware of some of the guards moving through the woods too. I catch the snapping of branches, but in the darkness, I can't see them.

"Cadence, but everyone who really knows me calls me Cade," I say, my arms relaxing enough that I slide one hand from his shoulder, up his neck and into his dark hair. Who knew I'd like being carried?

"Cadence. Nice. I like it. I'm Zane."

I'd like to say it's the first time that I've let a man inside me when I didn't know his name. But I will never forget Zane. Not his name, not the way his broad chest feels, or the way he carries me.

I don't normally like macho displays, but this feels different. It doesn't feel like posturing, its more…protection. It's a completely foreign feeling and I tuck it away, to think about later.

We clear the wooded trail, coming out of the trees and into another small clearing. Wooded areas like this are rare in this part of Nevada. This little oasis is fed by a river, which wraps behind three cottages that stand in an adorable little line. "What are those?" I suck in a breath as I take in the picturesque view bathed in moonlight.

"The one on the left…" he nods in its direction. "That is where we'll stay for the next three weeks."

I stare at the cottage, a calm washing through me. Just me, him, a river, and trees.

As long as I can keep it together for three weeks, this was a good decision, and for the first time tonight, I'm glad I came. Here I just might be able to think. Breathe. Relax.

It's a state I can't seem to sustain for longer than a day, so this will really be a totally different experience.

My fingers tighten in his hair. I'm not sure how I'll keep it together for that long without the restlessness creeping in. But Zane is amazing enough, that I'm going to try.

For the next three weeks, this is…home.

# CHAPTER THREE

CADENCE

ZANE CARRIES me into the house, kicking the door closed behind him. He lets go of me with one arm, supporting my weight with the other, before he flicks on a light.

I draw in the smallest gasp, as my head swivels around. The place is the perfect combination of homey and high-end.

The furniture looks expensive but comfortable, the kitchen full of top-of-the-line appliances and natural-stone countertops, but it's small enough to not be overwhelming.

A small hall leads off the main room and that's where Zane heads, me still in his arms. A door to the left reveals a medium-sized bedroom with a very large bed. Directly in front of us, a bathroom.

That's where he takes me, turning on another light, before he lowers me to the counter, setting me down on the cool stone. "Open your mouth."

"What?"

"I want to see what's bleeding. Open." It takes me a few seconds to adjust. I don't do well with direct commands, and my automatic response is to argue. But this man just saved me and he's trying to help me, so I part my lips unlocking my jaw without my usual arguing.

He looks inside, his brow furrowed. "Stick out your tongue."

I huff the smallest breath before I do as he's asked, using his inspection as an opportunity to assess the man I've agreed to spend the next twenty-one days with.

He's hot. Like, really, really hot.

Even better looking than I first thought. His dark hair is short on the back and sides, but the top is longer and styled in a side spike that only accentuates the square line of his jaw.

He's got gorgeous light gray eyes, strong cheekbones, and a crook in his nose that just makes him even more masculine.

I'm still wearing his tank top, so I've got a full view of all the muscles that ripple over his arms and down his chest leading to his six-pack abs.

"Your tongue's tip isn't severed. That's good." His eyes flick to mine and I forget to breathe.

I pull my tongue back into my mouth. "Good."

"Tongues heal quickly, you'll be fine." He reaches up to cup my cheek with his hand, brushing his finger over the bruised skin on my cheekbone. Then he looks at my neck where that fucker tried to bite me. He tips my head, inspecting the damage. "I was worried we'd be spending our first night together in the ER."

My jaw works as his words wash over me. Would he really have taken me to the ER? It's a really nice thought, but I doubt my own logic. Wouldn't he be more interested in collecting the spoils from his win?

I don't ask as he pushes back from the counter and then opens the shower door, leaning in to turn on the faucet.

The water pours from the rain-head shower, looking so inviting, I sigh. I'm covered in dirt and grime and I can't wait to wash it off.

Zane moves toward me again, wrapping his arms around me, and lifting me off the counter to bring me to my feet. "I'm going to undress you so I can check for any other injuries."

I quirk a single brow. "I thought you were undressing me because we're supposed to fuck."

His mouth twitches down into a frown. Does he not like the crassness of my words? I can have that effect.

"We only fuck when you want to fuck, Cadence. And between us, it will be something much deeper and better than fucking."

My mouth opens to respond when he reaches for the hem of his tank top, pulling it slowly over my head.

Then he takes off mine, adding it to his on the floor. Finally, he unsnaps my bra. I'm totally naked in front of him in the harsh light of the bathroom and I have to force myself not to curl my shoulders in. I don't do embarrassed.

His fingertips start at my neck, lightly running down my arms and then back up, tracing the plains of my body. His fingers are light, his touch so delicious that I lose myself in the feel of his hands, my head tipping back.

I turn when he instructs me to, his touch feels so good I forget myself and let him look all over my back. "Just a few bruises," he murmurs.

"Mm," is all I reply, wanting more of his hands on my skin. "Does that mean I can get in the shower?"

"It sure does."

"Are you joining me?" I look over my shoulder where he's bent down, inspecting a bruise on my leg.

"Do you want me to?"

We're still doing that permission thing? Part of me rebels. We're wasting time. But another parts of me likes it. It relaxes me. Here... with him...I'm safe. "Yes."

He's up in a second, kicking off his boots, shucking his pants down his powerful thighs. My mouth goes dry at the sight of those thighs and what's hanging between them.

That's all mine for the next three weeks.

If I don't blow the whole arrangement up, that is. Which I'll probably do, but that's a problem for some other point in time in the near future.

Tonight, I'm going to enjoy the spoils of war. My very own warrior.

I step into the hot spray, sighing at the feel of the water as rivulets of dirt wash down my skin.

Zane steps in behind me, grabbing the soap and brushing it over my skin. His hands slide over my body, running up my back and over my shoulders.

I arch into his touch, my hands extending out to give him more access as he washes down my sides and over my ass to scrub my legs.

The feel of his hands, the fact that's he crouched down, makes me throb with a need that steals my breath.

I can't remember ever feeling a desire this strong. The organizers of The Hunt were right about that. The competition has created this heightened sense of connection between us.

But I'm not even thinking about that now. I'd just take some really good sex.

And I already know it's going to be amazing with Zane.

My body follows the thought, my ass pushing back in clear invitation even as he reaches around, beginning to wash the front of my legs, then up my thighs to my hips and belly.

His hands slide over my ribs and then to my chest.

Like I said, I'm slender. Which means I don't have the biggest rack. In fact, they'd probably be classified as small. Sometimes I can fill a B cup but most of the time, I'm an A.

His hands, which are massive, swallow my bee stings, completely covering my boobs and a fair bit of my chest too.

My nipples peak against his palms even as he nuzzles my neck.

It's the first time he's touched me under the hot spray with anything other than tender efficiency.

I fall into the touch, pressing my back to his front, tilting my head to give him more access as I push my chest into his hands.

"You're going to get dirty again," he rumbles into my skin. "I haven't washed myself yet."

"I don't care," I answer, sliding my soapy ass over his pelvis. His thick cock swipes against my butt cheeks.

If my boobs are slight, but my ass is full—easily my best feature—and I use it to tempt and to invite.

He takes the invitation. His left hand leaves my chest to slide back down my belly to dip between my thighs. I'm so ready, that when his finger slides over my clit, I cry out, my whole body pulsing with the pleasure that radiates out from my core.

"Does my girl need me?" he rumbles in my ear.

"Yes," I cry back, pushing against his erection. This time, I don't care that he's asking again. It feels natural and a bit like dirty talk.

He moves his hand deeper between my legs, spreading me open as he bends his knees so that he can push back up inside me.

He feels so good, his thick cock filling me so full that he pushes on every nerve ending, and I'm shaking before he's even all the way inside me.

I lean toward the wall, my legs threatening to give out, but before I reach it, his arms tighten around me, holding my weight.

With the change in angle, he slides even deeper inside me, hitting me everywhere that feels good, and I let out this high-pitched gasp that doesn't even sound like me as I lose control of my body.

I'm so wrapped up in the pleasure, I don't notice my feet coming off the floor until they wrap around his calves, my weight one hundred percent held by him.

I've never had sex like this. Zane is this unique mix of tender and strong and it's like a drug. My every need and want is being met, where I'm so filled with pleasure, I'm not even aware of breathing.

I reach back, my hands fisting his hair, which causes my back to arch so that he's finally fully seated inside me.

He hits that spot I seriously thought was a myth and I scream out my pleasure, never wanting him to leave my body.

I flex my feet, causing the smallest movement of his cock, which rubs me in that perfect spot again, and my body hums as the sensation multiples.

We've hardly started and I'm already panting. "Zane," I beg, not even sure what I'm asking for. Faster? Harder? More?

But he knows.

Using the hand that's cupping my sex, he pushes me back off his cock, putting all the right pressure on my clit. And then he relaxes the arm, allowing me to slide back down his cock.

I tip my head forward, as my body shudders from the slide of his thick cock. My face dips into the spray, water filling my mouth and nose. I'm so lost I can't pay attention to breathing, apparently. But before I can correct, his biceps flex to pull me tighter to his chest, so that my face is back out of the water.

But I can't thank him as he hits my G-spot again, the trembling in my limbs redoubling.

"Oh. My. God," I gasp out as he lifts me again, pushing back into me faster this time. The extra speed causes the whole reaction to come at me quicker and I know I'm not going to make it very long.

He pumps into me again. Once. Twice. Three times and then I start to orgasm. It hits me with a force that steals my breath, the pleasure so intense I can't even speak, can't even push out a moan.

But he doesn't slow down. Now he's like a piston, pumping into me, causing a riot of fireworks to light inside me.

I finally scream out, every muscle in my body completely taut, as the pleasure overrides every other function.

He doesn't let up, though, slamming into me as I ride every ripple of pleasure. And then his own orgasm starts, a roar ripping from his throat as his body shudders, his cock jerking inside me.

It's gorgeous and I wish I could hold him, but I'm like limp spaghetti in his arms, so wrung out all I can do is close my eyes and just feel him.

He sags into my back and we both tip forward so that I'm pressed between his chest and the tile wall. "Wow," I manage to push out, the cooler surface feeling amazing against my cheek.

"You aren't kidding," he rasps into my neck, his hands splayed out on my skin.

"I'm not even sure I'll be able to walk after that." I'm joking. Mostly. Then again, I haven't tested my legs, which feel like jelly.

"Baby girl," he kisses up my neck to the sensitive spot just behind my ear, "I'll carry you any time you like."

I hum out my approval. I hope I can keep it together long enough to enjoy this man. Because I'm really going to lose something when I blow this up.

# CHAPTER FOUR

CADENCE

HE WASHES me again and then scrubs himself.

When we're done, we collapse into a super-comfortable bed. I curl around him, sighing out my contentment.

Is this what relationships are like for normal people? I'm warm and comfortable, his arm around my back as he holds me close. No man has ever held me like this. Or maybe I just never felt like this when they did.

But as I start to fall asleep, memories from tonight flit in and out of my thoughts.

Being under that fighter.

The helplessness of the attack.

I shake off the thoughts. I'm in bed with the man who protected me, and next to him, I'm safe.

But I don't love that thought either. Every time I rely on someone else, I end up…disappointed.

Still, I think Zane will keep me safe for the night. In the morning, everything will look different.

I fall asleep moments later, too tired to worry more. I have no idea how long I'm asleep when the dream starts.

I've had it before. I step into the pile-of-shit house that is our newest foster home. I'm late because I had to stay after and retake a math test that I failed.

But as I close the squeaky kitchen door, I hear Ava's sharp cry. And then our foster father yells, "Shut up."

The fight that always comes when Ava is in trouble bubbles up to the surface, dulling my reason and sharpening my senses. I can hear her struggle, the grunts and cries as I reach into the knife drawer and grab out an ice pick.

Gripping it in my palm, I sprint down the hall, stopping in our bedroom door.

And for a moment, I freeze. Because what I see...

It's Ava, her legs open, as our foster father ruts on top of her.

And then, it's me.

I'm no longer watching, I am Ava. Or I'm in Ava's position.

My chest restricts with fear, the cry of pain ripping from my lips.

"Cadence." A male voice penetrates the dream, mixes with it. "Cadence. Wake up."

My eyes burst open, but the dream is still my reality and as a face appears above me, I don't hesitate.

My hand balling into a fist, I strike out, popping him in the jaw with all the force my sleep-ladened muscles can muster.

It's enough.

His head snaps back, his hands flying to his face as he falls back on the mattress. "Jesus, Cadence. It's me."

I blink in complete confusion. "What?"

"It's Zane." He holds his face as he looks up at me where he lays flat on his back.

"Zane?" I draw in a shuddering breath, trying to make sense of where I am and what's happening, when the details start to filter back.

The Hunt. The shower. Going to bed. "Shit," I cry, scrambling up on my knees. "I'm so sorry. I was having a nightmare and..." He pulls his hand away and I see a bruise already blooming on his jaw. "Shit."

He shakes his head. "It's fine. I've suffered worse. Why don't you tell me what you were dreaming about?"

I freeze, my lips pressing shut. Honestly, his reaction is…weird. Who says punching me in the jaw is fine? No one. Psychopaths. "You can't actually mean that."

He shrugs. "You'd be surprised how many soldiers sleepwalk, sleep talk, and sleep fight. It's when they sleep shoot their weapons that you've got to be really careful."

I stare at him trying to process that one. This behavior is normal to him? I look down, realizing I'm completely naked and now up on my knees.

Shaking my head, I don't cover myself, it's a sign of weakness, as I push from the bed. "Know where my clothes might be?"

"In the drawers," he points to the bureau on the far wall.

I walk over, opening a drawer, and then another, until I find an oversized sleep shirt and pull it on. Covered, I turn back to him. "Where are your clothes?"

He shrugs. "In my bag on the floor."

"How come mine are unpacked and yours aren't?"

"Because your stay was definite. Mine was not." He stands up, also naked, as he crosses his arms over his chest. "What was your dream about?"

I sigh, not wanting to share the details of my past. "None of your business."

"It is my business."

"Why is that?" I start for the door, then, heading out to the kitchen. I could use a glass of water and he's going to need some ice. But I'm also running from his questions. It's way too soon to introduce him to my crazy.

"Because you're my woman."

I stop, turning back to him. "We've known each other for a few hours." I hold back adding, *That's stupid.*

"That's irrelevant."

"It's not." My arms cross as I glare. I'm not sure if it's the dream or the fact my past feels so close to the surface. The one where no one ever stayed. No one wanted me when they realized the giant bags I carried with me, and I'm not talking about actual luggage.

For the record, I didn't have any. I carried my shit in a black trash bag.

"When I signed up for The Hunt, I made a commitment to you. That I'd be what you needed."

My glare turns to a look of complete confusion. "But you didn't know me."

"Doesn't matter."

I roll my eyes. This is the dumbest conversation I've ever had. Opening the freezer, I grab some ice from the bin, placing it in a towel before I hand it to him. "For your face."

"Thank you." He takes the ice, placing it on his jaw. "But rest assured, the bruise was not from you but from earlier this evening."

"Oh," my shoulders sag as I start searching for a glass. "That's a relief."

He's quiet, like he's considering my words, before he asks. "So, what was your dream about?"

"You're not a quitter, I'll give you that."

"Nope."

I don't like talking about my past, and I don't usually share much of it with anyone. Not the guys I date, not people I meet at work, or anyone I end up hanging with socially. It's easier that way.

And I know I'm here to change some old habits, but I don't think finding out about my fucked-up childhood is going to make him like me more. Still, I can give him a few details. "It's nothing. My friend was attacked, and I walked in on it happening."

"Attacked? Attacked how?" He asks, his voice taking on this menacing tone. The towel of ice hits the counter with a thump.

I shake my head. "It doesn't matter. Ava, that's my friend, she's not a fighter, which makes her vulnerable."

"And so, you do the fighting for both of you," he rumbles, his brow slashing into an angry line.

He's not wrong. But I don't want to get into Ava, because it's another topic that makes me look bad. While she does rely on me to be the fighter, she's the everything else. Stable. Reliable. Kind. She's bailed me out of more scrapes than I can count.

I'm the shitty friend who didn't tell her I was coming here because I knew she'd try and talk me out of it. And because she needs a jolt to realize I'm not worth all her good.

I find a glass and turn on the faucet, filling it with water and then I take a long swallow.

"What time is it?" I ask, after I've taken several swallows.

"Four."

"In the morning?" Of course it's the morning. I dump the rest of the water back down the sink and then place the glass in the dishwasher. "We should probably go back to bed."

He picks up the towel of ice and steps up next to me, still completely naked, as he opens the towel and drops the ice in the sink.

My eyes drift down, the sight of his twig and berries making me ache all over again.

"We should," he answers, setting the towel on the counter as he hooks my waist. "Need help falling back to sleep?" The look in his eyes leaves no question to what he's referring. Thank goodness the talking portion of this wake up is over and we can get back to the good stuff.

I nip at my lip. "I thought you'd never ask."

He chuckles, bending low to wrap his hand under my ass and lifts me in the air. I let out a breathless little giggle as I grasp the back of his head. "I can walk."

"Why bother?" he responds with a devilish glint in his eyes. "I like carrying you."

I like it too. And that could be a problem.

# CHAPTER FIVE

ZANE

MY GIRL IS SPOOKED.

She played off that dream like it wasn't a big deal, but I know trauma when I see it.

She's faced more than her fair share and she's developed a hard outer shell to protect her wounds.

So many soldiers do the same. During the day, they wear their strength like a bulletproof vest, but at night…

I went to medical school, paid for by the federal government, in exchange for my service. My skill took me to Special Ops, where I provided medical care on covert missions.

But now, I've left the forces and I'm ready to start on my civilian life. I'd been delaying settling down until after I retired.

Absent husbands don't make for good partners, in my opinion. And I stand by that statement.

The problem, I realized after I left, was that I'm a different man now. I've seen some of the worst of life, been through hell, and every woman I've tried to date, just wasn't…deep enough.

It's not that I want my woman to have suffered. But I also can't spend Friday nights getting drunk at Applebee's and then get up on Saturday morning to pick out curtains at Bed Bath and Beyond.

I need more.

And after a year and a half of trying and failing to meet a woman with strength and character, and an understanding of what a life spent in pursuits other than just fun might look like, I decided to flip the script and try this.

There are no guarantees beyond the next few weeks. Cadence could decide I'm not for her. I could decide there is only more pain on this path, not more merit, and we could go our separate ways.

But while I'm here, I will be fully present for Cadence. And no matter how this goes, I want her to be better for knowing me.

With that in mind, I carry her back into the bedroom, her body warm and soft next to mine.

Cadence is, hands down, the most beautiful woman I've ever laid eyes on. She must have done some modeling with her face and figure.

Flawless features are crowned with shiny red hair that is like fire, and large brown eyes. Her pale pink lips are perfectly bowed, though she tries to set her features in strong lines, the warm brown depths of her large eyes betray her vulnerability.

She talks tough, she acts tough too, but the way her hands rest on my body when I carry her. They beg me to hold her tightly.

I do.

One hand sliding over the lush curve of her ass, I settle my other arm across her back, keeping her steady and secure.

The more I pleasured her in the shower, the deeper she sank into me, until she let me be her…everything.

Her strength. Her pleasure. Her heat.

Her chest is pressed against my face and I kiss her on her breastbone, nuzzling into her. "You smell fantastic."

She scoffs. "I smell like sleep."

She's a tough nut, I'll give her that. And yes, she does smell like sleep, but the smell is pleasing to some back-of-the-brain sense I can't name.

I don't need to. However, I might describe it, one-word echoes through my attempts: right. She smells right.

I kiss her chest through the fabric of the shirt she's pulled on. "Whatever it is, I like it."

She scoffs like my words are ridiculous, but her hands give her away. They spread out on my shoulders, sliding up my neck and into my hair.

I smile into her shirt, as I navigate around the bed, gently laying her down on the mattress.

The sex is plenty hot without getting frantic. My first job is to establish some trust. Then I can learn about the trauma.

She's naked under the shirt, no underwear, and I take full advantage as I begin kissing down her body, pulling up the hem of the shirt.

She hums out her approval when my lips meet the bare skin of her belly.

Her legs fall open as I trace her hips, the slender curve of them looking so small in my large hands.

Her pale skin glows in the moonlight as I kiss that spot where her stomach meets her legs. She lets out a breathless giggle.

I love the sound of it.

To be honest, I'm not a man who likes giggly women. But Cadence isn't one of those. She rarely laughs like that, I can tell, which makes the sound so sweet. I nip playfully at the same spot, making a full laugh break from her lips as she curls into the mattress.

I laugh too. A little playfulness is exactly what we need.

I start kissing closer to her mound, lightly licking and sucking as I move, tasting her skin, getting to know her.

There is no giggling now as her body arches into my touch, her stomach curling in and her hips flexing up in an unspoken invitation.

I don't hesitate.

Cadence is sporting a Brazilian, and while I love the view, my preference is a more natural look.

Still, I can't deny the merits as I kiss across her bare mound, nothing holding back the smell of her arousal or the flush turning her pale skin pink as her lips swell with her desire.

I drag my teeth lightly over her mound, just creating a little more sensation. She moans, her legs spreading wider.

I know an opportunity when I see one, which is why I dip lower, circling my tongue over her clit.

Her body jolts as a keening cry fills the room.

I start working her clit, pressing a finger inside her. Her thighs tremble around my face, her heels digging into the small of my back.

Starting a rhythm, it isn't long before she buries her fingers into my hair, tugging on the strands and pulling me closer.

I can already tell Cadence likes a bit of pain with her pleasure. But we are wading into those waters slowly and carefully.

Too often, triggers are buried inside desires and it's a razor's edge. I will always err on the side of safe.

If there is one thing I want her to feel, it's that. I can do a complicated woman as long as those complications don't keep us from building intimacy.

Which is why I don't go harder, just steady, as I add a second finger, feeling her stretch around me.

She stutters through a gasp, grinding against my hand. She's wide open now, dripping wet, her heels digging so hard into the small of my back that she's almost forcing me up her body.

"Zane," she gasps. "Zane, it's so good, but I want…" Her words drift off as her chest arches up into the air, her head tossed back, her long red hair streaming across the bed.

"What do you want, sweetheart?" I say, coming up for air and enjoying the gorgeous view.

"Your cock," she gasps, tugging on my hair as she tries to pull me up.

She doesn't have to ask me twice.

Sliding up her body, she pushes me along with her feet. My cock finds her opening, sinking inside her, making us both groan.

I've been going slowly. Careful. But as I sink inside her, her hands reach around me, grabbing my ass and squeezing us tighter together, and I lose my careful control.

Pulling out, I thrust back inside her, setting a pace that has both of us fighting for air as we climb higher and higher, our hips coming together as I use all my strength to drive her wild.

She scratches at my skin, her mouth crashing into mine as our tongues tangle together.

My balls are on fire with the effort not to cum, but I hold out for her, knowing that she's close. Her body trembles under mine, her pants and high-pitched moans only adding to the fever, until finally she breaks. She cries my name into my mouth and it's all the permission I need to let go and cum like I'd die if I didn't.

I have no idea if Cadence and I will work, but I know that sex has never been this good.

I don't stop pumping until we're both completely spent. Cadence's arms have gone soft around me, her cheek nuzzling into the space between my shoulder and neck. "That was..."

I kiss her again, soft and slow. I'm too gassed to speak and I just need a minute before I'm going to be able to settle us properly in the bed.

Her eyes flutter closed, her body twitching as she falls asleep.

"Cade?"

"Hmm," she hums between her closed lips.

I push up on my elbows looking down at her gorgeous face, so relaxed in sleep. She looks younger, even more vulnerable. It makes me think of the dream and what she might have gone through when she was young and innocent. "Where were you and Ava when you walked in on her being attacked?"

Her eyes flutter open, the pain in them undeniable. "At our foster parents' shit run down shithole of a two-bedroom ranch."

Foster parents? Did she grow up in foster care? How bad was it? But I don't ask. At least not now. She's already drifting back to sleep, so instead, I wrap her in my arms and lift her up to settle her head on the pillow and tuck her body under the covers.

Then I curl around her and say with my body what I don't with my words. *With me, you are safe.*

She snuggles down into my embrace, letting out a soft sigh.

Tonight, she sleeps. Tomorrow, I'll ask more questions.

But I can already tell she's not going to like giving answers. If this is going to work, however, I've got a find a way past her hard shell.

# CHAPTER SIX

CADENCE

I WAKE to bright sunlight filtering in through the windows of the bedroom. Reaching behind me, I press my hand to empty sheets. Zane is gone. Lifting my head, the view out the bank of windows instantly makes me smile. The river babbles away as the sun sparkles off the blue water.

Man, I could get used to this.

I stretch, my shirt falling back down my torso. Zane had pushed it up my chest when we came back to bed, and that's where it stayed.

The orgasm in the shower had been fantastic, but the one in the middle of the night…it was unreal. I never imagined sex could feel like that.

I hear the clatter of metal coming from the kitchen and then the smell of coffee hits my nose.

It pushes me out of bed, and into the bathroom where my toothbrush sits in a little holder.

I brush my teeth and use the bathroom to freshen up before I step out into the kitchen.

Zane stands at the stove, putting bacon in a pan. He's shirtless with a pair of low-slung sweatpants barely hanging onto his hips.

"Brave," I say with a small laugh.

He looks back at me, a sexy smile playing on his lips. "What's that?"

"Cooking bacon shirtless."

He joins me in the laughter. "I like a little danger with my breakfast."

I wrinkle my nose, as he leans to the right and grabs a mug from the cabinet.

"Coffee?" he asks, holding up the mug.

"Yes, please," I murmur, stepping forward.

He pours out some from the pot on the counter. "Milk? Sugar?"

"Black," I answer reaching out my hands.

"Really? You sure you weren't in the armed forces?"

I take the mug from his hand, taking a big swig of the dark brew. I'm not much for breakfast, but I can't live without my cup of coffee. "I'm sure."

"How did you find black coffee then?"

I shrug as I turn away. I know it's tough that he can't even ask me about coffee without me tensing up. But it's a sensitive subject.

Every bit of food was a resource in most of the placements I was put in.

Most foster homes didn't feed me breakfast. Or dinner. Lunch came at school when I had it.

Coffee, however, came in a giant can and it was one of the few things I just got to have. Somedays I survived on only caffeine to keep me going.

Even milk and sugar were frequently rationed unless it was powdered. "Coffee is perfect all on its own."

He cocks his head, studying me. I don't like it.

Zane can learn how to play my body like a fiddle. But my mind? No thank you.

"Most people add loads of cream and sugar to dull the actual taste. Black coffee is usually an acquired taste."

I shrug, taking a big sip.

Zane stares at me for another minute before the bacon starts to sizzle and then he turns back to the stove.

He works at the stove while I drink the coffee, pouring myself another mug.

That's when he puts the bacon on the small island that acts as an eating area and a prep space. "Help yourself."

"No, thanks," I answer, taking the first sip of my second cup.

"No thanks?" he squints at me. "Not hungry yet?"

I shrug, straightening up in a fighting pose. I know I shouldn't be fighting over bacon, but he's hit this nerve and my hackles are rising. "Nope."

He cocks his head. "Should I wait another hour before I make the eggs?"

I shake my head. "I don't need eggs. Thanks."

His eyes narrow. "When do you plan to eat?"

"None of your business." The words are out of my mouth before I've thought them through, but I notch my chin just the same.

He slowly sets the spatula down. "None of my business?"

"I'm a grown-ass woman. I don't need you to tell me when to eat."

His arms cross over his chest as he grows taller before my eyes. I'm not the only one who knows how to strike a pose.

My spine straightens to match his energy as I glare over the rim of my coffee cup.

"You fought two grown men last night, went to bed really late, and then we had, at least for me, mind-blowing sex. Twice. Why wouldn't you give your body some fuel?"

My shoulders drop a fraction of an inch. Because that's actually kind of sensible. But I don't need him to tell me when to eat. "I can take care of myself."

He cocks his head to the side. "Are you always like this?"

"Like what?" But my fingers curl into the cup, because he's zeroing in on one of the ways I'm prickly.

"So resistant to letting people help you?"

My mouth opens in surprise. How did he figure that out so quick? But I snap my teeth closed. "No."

His brow lifts, but he turns back to the stove, cracking an egg into the pan. Silently, I reach over to the plate and take a piece of bacon, popping the whole thing in my mouth before he can see what I've done.

I can admit he's right without telling him. I don't want him to think he gets to boss me around. He doesn't…

Not ever.

The distance between us lasts until Zane sits down to a large plate of bacon and eggs. I nearly ask him to make me one but then change my mind. I do snatch another piece of bacon when he's not looking.

Then I flounce off the shower.

The rest of the day passes much more pleasantly. We wade in the river, discuss safer topics like our favorite color.

Though, honestly, even that one holds pain for me.

I'm starting to realize why I so quickly detonate every relationship.

Apparently, I'm a field of land mines.

"Let me see," Zane says as he immerses himself in the two-foot-deep water, only his head above the surface. "I went through a green phase as a child, then blue. I nearly drove my dad crazy repainting my room."

I feel the tug, one I haven't let pull at my chest for years. I wanted to be one of those kids that had parents who would decorate their room with them. I'd be lying on some stained mattress in a shit crack house and I'd dream about a pretty pink room with lace curtains, and a canopy, and a mom who read me a story and tucked me in.

I carried the fantasy with me when I moved into every shitty little musty-smelling bedroom in my string of foster homes. I look away, letting my legs float down river. "And what color did you finally land on?"

"Camo," he answers with an easy smile. "What about you?"

"I'm a red girl," I say with a shrug. I don't share that pink was my first fantasy or about how my favorite jacket was red. I got it when I was fourteen at a thrift store and took it through five different placements and then to my first job interview at a local diner. It was my first piece of armor that gave me confidence.

I got the job but blew it up three weeks later when I stole from the register after the boss screamed at me for messing up an order.

"I can totally see you as a red girl."

"Oh yeah, why's that?" I flip on my side to meet his eyes.

"Flaming hair, dark eyes, temper. Red suits you."

That makes me smile. "Yeah. I guess it does." I let the water pull me downstream a bit. "So, why'd you join the military?"

His smile slips. "My dad died. I didn't have money for med school."

I'm silent for a second, processing that one. "I'm sorry about your dad." But I didn't miss the fact that med school was mentioned.

"Thanks. It's been twelve years, and it hurts a lot less than it used to."

I nod. "What about med school?"

"I went, thanks to the GI Plan."

"Wait," I stare at him my eyes going wide. "You're Dr. Zane?"

He smiles again. "'Fraid so. Though they usually call me Dr. Phillips. The military paid for the degree and then I served as a medical professional when I graduated."

My eyes cast down. I barely graduated high school. Mostly because of my behavior. I was smart enough. Which is just more evidence this thing with Zane is very temporary. I'm not the girl who lands a doctor. I should have known...

Planting my feet, I stand, wading out of the water before I wrap myself in a towel. "I'm hungry. I'm going to get something to eat."

I came here for change. A chance to step outside my fucked-up life and try to find a future. But there is no way this is working out.

Zane gets out too, coming up behind me. "What would you like?"

"I've got it," I answer, slipping on my flip-flops before I start for the cabin.

"Are we back to that?"

"To what?" I ask, huffing out a breath.

"This food thing. You get very resistant..."

The words fly out of my mouth before I think about them. "When people starve you, you learn not to let anyone control your food—" I stop, realizing what I'm saying. What the fuck is wrong with me? I never say shit like that.

It's like my every wound has come to the surface.

But his eyes go wide as he reaches out a hand to me. I slap it away before I turn. I'm too raw, I don't want to touch or be touched.

I start for the cabin, but I hear him following. "What?" I turn again, my hands coming to my hips as I glare.

He stops too, assessing me slowly. "You were in foster care with your friend, right?"

"Yeah."

"Did she get treated like that too?" he asks.

I have no idea what he's building toward. "Yeah. Of course."

"Does she struggle with this kind of thing too?"

"No. Of course not." Ava had a real mom for the first eight years of her life who cared for her. Loved her. Most of her issues revolve around her attack.

"Did Ava take your food?"

"What? No. Do I look like the kind of person that a five-foot-four-petite blonde could take from?"

That makes his brows lift.

I sigh out my frustration, not really wanting to talk about Ava. "She's not weird about people making food for her. And she doesn't have anger issues either. But she doesn't date. That's her issue."

His jaw drops. "Like ever?"

"Never. She wants to wrap herself around me like a boa constrictor instead." I turn back toward the cabin, wincing about what I just said. It's kind of true. But also, not fair. She's given me every part of herself in return. And if anything, my issues mess with her life way more than hers do with mine.

I'm not healthy for her. I'm a shit friend, one. And two, she needs someone to help her see that not all men are like our bastard foster father. I'm not exactly modeling healthy dating experiences.

"I see. You need more space than that."

Is he trying to figure me out? Fuck that. Like I need to see the reflection of this hot mess in his eyes.

# CHAPTER SEVEN

Cadence

Zane gives me space for the rest of the day, which I appreciate. By the time night falls, I'm ready to go to bed with him and enjoy the benefits of being here.

I brush my teeth and wash my face and then slip into a cute little black nightie that I packed on a whim.

But after a day of being standoffish, I think I might have to give him a few indicators that I'm ready to resume our intimacy. And by that, I mean sex. Mind-blowing sex.

I hear him in the bathroom and arrange myself on the bed with a hip up, my legs on full display.

He walks into the bedroom and stops. "Well, hello."

"Hi," I give him a sexy smile and my best come-hither stare.

He shrugs off his shirt, tossing it to the floor. My smile grows as I rub my knees together, getting ready for all the bliss that's coming.

He pulls off his athletic pants, folding them and setting them on the bureau so that he's in nothing but boxer briefs and then he turns out the light.

Moving back to the bed, he climbs in and pulls the covers up his body. And then…he turns his back to me.

My brow furrows as I stare at the back of his head. "What the hell?"

"I could ask you the same," he replies, sounding neither upset nor hurt.

"What does that mean?" I huff, but the pang in my gut tells me that I already know.

"We're not here for meaningless sex, Cadence. That was never what this was about. If that's what you want, you can get that anywhere else and so can I. It's not what I'm interested in from you."

He's right. I know he is. But I've never been one to deny a good fight just because I was wrong.

I came here for a change and instantly fell into old patterns again the moment real intimacy and sharing started developing.

Hell, all he had to do was ask a couple of questions…

"I've got news for you, I've had my fair share of sex, and it never feels like this," I say my hand coming to my hip.

He turns over to look at me, his face deadly calm, but his eyes are…resolute. "That's because we share a bond from the competition. A bond you are doing your best to kill."

My chin notches as I glare back. "I'm trying to kill it? You're the one who's prying into my past and bossing me around. Why don't we try it in the reverse, huh? Why don't I start telling you when and what to eat or ask you the uncomfortable questions that dig into your worst memories?"

I see his slight wince and know I've landed a good shot. "I didn't mean to ask more than you were ready to give. And I only asked you to eat because—"

I push up from the bed, staring down at him because it helps me hold onto my anger. "Foster homes are frequently light on food. Maybe you get two meals a day, maybe you only get one. You eat what they tell you when they tell you and thank them for a gas station burrito warmed up in the communal microwave." I don't even know why I'm saying this.

His jaw hardens as he pushes up. "Cadence, that is—"

"I don't need your pity. I don't. I just want you to understand that I don't let anyone tell me what to eat or when."

"I don't pity you," he shakes his head as he comes to stand next to me. "But that doesn't mean I can't be sad for the little girl who didn't get everything that she needed."

His words make me want to cry, which in turn, pisses me off. Anger is the only way I know to protect myself from the hurt. "I am fine. Just fine. And just so we're clear, the person not giving me what I need right now, is you."

"I disagree," he rumbles back.

"Oh yeah, why's that?"

"Because what you need is a connection with a person that is deeper than sex." He's raising himself up again, arms crossed over his chest.

"I decide what I need, not you." I poke him in the chest to make my point. "You're a bossy asshole, you know that?"

"Fine. I want a connection with a person that's deeper than sex. And I was hoping that person would be you, but if I can't even suggest you eat breakfast without you shutting down, that's going to be difficult."

My hands clench into fists. It's not like I didn't know this would happen. "Well then why don't you just fuck off." My voice rises with every word.

"That's going to be productive. You telling me to fuck off instead of working through a problem."

"Sorry. How about you fuck the fuck off." Now I'm screaming, as my hands ball into fists.

He steps closer. "Listen, I'm not asking for too much here and you—"

But I don't want to hear more, and I give him a good shove backwards. "I don't do men crowding me."

His jaw goes granite hard. "Crowding you? Have you lost your mind?"

My mind totally buzzes with emotion as I feel the rage burn through me. "You're calling me crazy?"

"No. Not crowding you. And not calling you crazy. It's an expression. I'm just trying to figure out how this day went so wrong."

I shake my head, realizing that I've gotten to the same place I do every time, only in record time. The Hunt didn't get me past my issues, it only shortened my timeline. Spinning on a heel, I stomp out to the living room and open the front door as Zane appears in the entrance of the bedroom.

Seeing him just pisses me off more and makes me ache all at the same time. Instead of saying that, I toss over my shoulder, "I'm a fucked-up woman with a fucked-up past and intimacy issues. Now you know." And then I step out into the night in bare feet and a scrap of satin before I slam the door shut.

I look across the dark woods, the river sparkling in the moonlight. I loved this place less than twenty-four hours ago. Now…

I just want to escape.

The grounds are surrounded by a wall. I don't know how big this place is exactly, but I know I'm only going so far.

Still, I can't go back in there.

He said shit. I said even shittier shit. I know I'm not spending the next few weeks sleeping outside. Maybe tomorrow I can get my phone and tell the organizers I need to leave.

But for tonight…

I'm stuck outside. My pride will allow nothing less.

I can already feel that I've messed this all up. From sleeping outside in a tiny nightie, to screaming my past at Zane, I'm doing my best to ruin this whole thing. I'm sure I just succeeded.

I step on a rock and hiss in a breath, lifting my foot. "Shit," I gasp, as I hop up and down.

"Cadence," Zane says from behind me.

I spin, holding in another gasp of surprise. "What the—"

"Sorry," he mumbles. "I didn't mean to scare you. Sneaking is a professional hazard of Special Ops."

I want to tell him I hate him, and that sneaking up is a terrible thing to do to a frightened woman. But before I can get the words out, he's sweeping me into his arms.

"What are you doing?"

"You can be mad at me inside."

"You're not hearing me, don't tell me what to do."

He sighs. "I'm hearing you. I'll sleep on the couch. Or outside if you prefer. I'm rather adept at using a rock as a pillow, another skill thanks to the military. But either way, you can be furious with me in the bed and not outside with hardly any clothes on and no shoes."

"Oh." That is actually really nice. And the fact that he's still willing to do that for me almost makes me sorry I said all the things I said.

My arms wrap about his neck as he carries me into the house. There is still a part of me that wants to tell him I can take care of myself, that I'll sleep outside if I want to, but I've burned out a bunch of the anger, and now I just feel tired. Low.

Besides, he's right.

One of us sleeping on the couch is a way more sensible solution. And the fact that he's giving me the choice to kick him out.... "I've got a real temper," I say softly.

"Always?" he asks.

"What does that mean?"

"Like did you have it as a small child, or did it develop later?"

I blink a few times. "Later, actually."

He doesn't say more as he opens the door and once again carries me into the cabin.

Not that it's even close to the same as when we stepped over the threshold last night.

He closes the door and starts for the bedroom. "If you're thinking that it doesn't matter when my anger issues surfaced, just that they're too much, I wouldn't blame you."

He stops in the middle of the living room. "You aren't too much, Cadence. I like a little fight."

"Fight?" My brows lift as he enters the bedroom.

"What I know I don't want is a woman who spends all her time telling me about her latest shopping trip, or her decorating plans, or…" He looks up at the ceiling. "How she's already mapped out the perfect wedding."

My insides go completely soft because I have never been one of those girls.

"You're not going to scare me off because you're a little complicated."

"Really?" I swallow down a lump, wanting his words to be true.

"I've seen some dark shit, Cade. It's made me darker. It's not that I don't want a bright future, I do. But I just need it with someone who might understand, not a woman who just wants a J. Crew cutout."

"Oh," I say and then I pull myself up by his neck to kiss his lips. It's just a small kiss, not sexual.

It's meant as a thank you. No one has ever said something like that to me before. "I know I need to let some of the anger go. But it's the only thing that kept me safe for so long, you know?"

I've never shared that with a single person, and it feels good to say it now.

"Yeah." And then he kisses me. It's long and slow and full of tenderness and promise.

# CHAPTER EIGHT

ZANE

CADENCE IS PUTTY in my arms now, her body pliant as she molds to me.

The second she walked out the door I knew two things.... First, my girl has been really hurt—and she is my girl—but second, I'm getting her back with the understanding she's going to need some patience and love to heal.

I've got both.

I softly part her lips, my tongue sliding against hers as I hold her tightly in my arms. I'm not trying to seduce her. This kiss is meant to tell her that I'm still here.

Her fingers curl into my hair before she pulls back only far enough to say, "Let's go to bed."

I don't need another invitation as I start moving again, pushing into the bedroom and laying her on the covers.

The little nightie she's got on is silky and hugs her slender body as it slides over her skin.

I trace her curves, one knee on the bed as I bend down to plunder her mouth, tasting her over and over.

I'm determined to go slower tonight. This is meant to be lovemaking, not just sex, but our mouths grow hungrier and hungrier as she starts tugging on my hair to pull me closer.

I smile against her lips.

Cadence doesn't lack in intensity and I love that about her.

At some point, we'll discuss professional counseling. She's a child of neglect and abuse, those are wounds that run too deep for just patience to cure.

But the chemistry between us is too strong to ignore, and I've always been a man who's been up for a challenge.

And what I see under Cadence's anger is a woman of strength and grit who could love with an intensity that would steal a man's heart.

She keeps tugging me closer and I heed her pressure.

Her legs naturally part, my body settling between hers, her legs locking around the back of mine.

I'm trying to take this slow, to show Cadence this is about more than sex for me. It's about building something stronger and more real.

But her passion can sweep a man down river, and before I know it, our hips are grinding together, my chest sliding over the silk of her lingerie.

I pull at the straps, freeing her breasts as I kiss down her neck, wanting to taste more of her skin.

She arches into me, so open I know I need to get us to the same place emotionally. When we're on the same page, it's magic.

I reach her breasts and suck one of her nipples into my mouth.

Cadence cries out, the nipple peaking against my tongue as her fingernails dig into my neck.

Cadence made a few good points today. Her well of pain runs deep, and we might need more warm-up time before I dig into it.

I can accept that.

Her feet slide up the back of my thighs, over my ass, before she works her toes into the waistband of my boxer briefs.

I've barely rumbled out my approval when she starts pulling the elastic down my hips using only her feet.

I lift up to help her, my cock springing free as the cloth settles around my thighs.

So much for making tender love.

Her nightie is around her waist, my underwear at my thighs when I plunge inside her, both of us groaning out our satisfaction.

She feels so good, her slick heat wrapped around my cock as her legs lock around my waist.

I bury my face in her neck, drawing in her scent. "Cadence," I groan out, wanting to explain. But I can't, I don't have the words to describe why this is so different.

So instead, I gather her close, kissing her skin even as I pull out and plunge back in. Her hips meet mine, her lips pressing to my temple. "Zane," she cries out, sounding pained. Almost frightened.

"I'm here," I whisper into her skin, kissing up her neck and over her jaw until my lips touch hers. "I'm not going anywhere."

"Promise?" she asks and then I see the fear in her eyes. It makes my chest so tight, I can't breathe. Is that why she pushes me away? Because she's afraid I'll leave?

I take that as a challenge.

I'm not going anywhere. "Promise." I mean the word. I'm starting to understand Cadence and when she's going to be tough. But I'm tough too.

I pull out and push back in, picking up the pace until we're both moaning, getting so close that I squeeze my eyes shut, holding off, as Cadence's pussy tightens like a vise.

Her fingers are frantic on my skin until she finally screams my name, breaking. The ripples of her orgasm unleash mine as I groan out my finish.

I collapse on top of her, gathering her close. Her arms wrap tight around my neck. "I'm not easy to like."

I lift my head, prying my eyes open. "Who told you that?" Her words don't scare me off. They make me ache for her.

"Trust me. I just know it." She looks away and then I see them. Tears.

A man brutally attacked her yesterday and she didn't cry. She's not a person who shows vulnerability often. This wound runs deep.

"You need to give yourself more credit than that." I frame her face in my hands, wanting her to understand. She's got so much good.

"You want the truth, ask Ava. She'll tell you. I hurt everyone who tries to get close to me. If you're smart, Zane, you'll quit now before it's too late."

I kiss her mouth, but mentally, I make a note. I'm not going to ask Ava how Cadence is bad. I'm going to ask Ava what she did to hurt Cadence so bad. Because clearly Cadence's best friend is as bad for her as all those foster parents.

And that conversation is going to happen. But not tonight. Tonight, it's my job to tell her, show her, I'm here for her and I'm not going anywhere.

# CHAPTER NINE

CADENCE

THE NEXT WEEK passes with a harmony that feels like a deep, long exhale.

I'm not sure I've ever relaxed like this. Zane cooks for me regularly, we eat, sleep, swim, and play.

There is no other word for it. From wrestling, to walking, to laughing, we just enjoy each other's company.

I've never been so content in my own head. I don't seek conflict, don't search for ways to push him away. And I slowly feel the deep wound of hurt I carry begin to heal in a way I've never imagined.

He keeps asking me questions about my past. Some I answer, some I don't, and when I don't, he doesn't press.

But I do tell him about my mom, and how she was an addict. We're out walking the property, staying in the shade of the trees.

I only share a few of the memories of sleeping in crack houses. "How old were you?"

I shake my head. "Young."

"Drugs are a hard habit to kick and it can span generations," he says, giving me a sidelong glance. Is he asking about my own proclivities?

"I tried drinking and drugs in my teens and early twenties. But I'm done with that." I turn toward him, meeting his eye. "I've got enough problems without adding addiction."

"You don't drink at all?"

I shake my head. "Is that weird for you?"

"No," he answers. "I don't really drink either. Medical school was too strenuous, and field work was too dangerous for that kind of indulgence."

I lace my fingers through his. Because it's the first time I've thought that I might suit him. Sobriety is something we share, something I bring when other women might not.

It makes me warm inside and I bump my shoulder against his in a playful move as I bite my lip.

He responds by scooping me up and spinning me around.

I can't believe I told him about my horrendous childhood and now he's spinning me around instead of tossing me out.

I've always thought my past made me inferior. I know it's not my fault, but that doesn't mean it makes me less desirable.

I didn't grow up being taught to match curtains with sofas. Then again, Zane says that he's not interested in that woman.

My entire life has taught me that his feelings won't last. But for the first time in a very long time, I'm buoyed by hope. It scares the crap out of me.

Every person I've trusted has quit on me. Except for Ava…

Are there really two people in this world who can care about me even though I'm the prickliest pear ever?

If I'm honest, I've done my damnedest to push Ava away. In fact, my eyes flutter closed as I delve deeper. I've been examining thoughts this week I've shied away from for years.

I'd assumed all this time something was wrong with her that she still loved me.

That it's her wound that keeps her by my side, and not my worth.

"What's wrong?" Zane rumbles.

"Nothing. Just thinking about Ava."

"Ava," he growls back.

I furrow my brow, trying to understand what he means. "Every time I talk about Ava you seem angry."

"I know you say she's your friend but—"

"But what?" I ask as he gently sets me on my feet.

"But she seems connected to every one of your most traumatic experiences."

"Yeah. Cause she was there. For all intents and purposes, she's my sister. We lived that shit together."

His brow furrows. "But you've had to hurt yourself to save her."

"What does that mean?"

"You stabbed a man to protect her, Cadence. That's a wound you carry on your soul."

I stare at him. "Does it bother you that I've done things like that?" My throat closes as I brace myself for the rejection I know is coming. But somehow, for the first time in my adult life, the idea of it doesn't make me angry, just sad.

I don't rise to fight. I don't hide from the pain.

I won't use anger to protect myself against Zane. I can't. I'll feel it all this time. I really have rewritten some of my shit patterns.

"No. You can't imagine the shit I did in the military. It bothers me you've suffered for her."

My mouth drops open as I try to understand. This is not the conversation I thought we'd be having. "You don't understand."

"Then tell me."

"Ava lives in the shittiest little apartment, despite having an amazing job. She saves all her money."

"Okay?"

"Three times she's used that money to help me get sober by paying for rehab," I whisper, knowing that Zane is going to understand why he shouldn't trust me. "She's bailed me out of prison. Gotten me jobs. She's..." I feel tears well in my eyes. "She's the only person who has ever loved me."

"But..." He starts, but I raise my hand.

"If anything, someone should be giving her this lecture. About how I'm a bad influence. One of the reasons I left is because…I'm dragging her down. Not the other way around."

I steel my spine as I gather myself to say the next words. "And if you're smart, you'll see that I would drag you down too." I drop my head, tears misting my eyes. I've said the truth. The words that weigh heavy on my heart.

When I take the anger away, I know that I've used it to push people away so that I don't have to face this moment. Admitting they're right to leave me behind.

That I deserve rejection.

"You're not dragging me down. I…" And that's when I hear the pain in his voice.

My chin snaps up. "What is it?"

"Umm…" He winces then, and I blink back my surprise as I try to determine where this conversation is heading.

"What?" I snap.

"Ava's been calling a lot," he quietly answers. "Last night she called while you were in the shower, and I picked up."

"Okay…" My chest grows tight. Because what I did to Ava, coming here without telling her was shitty. I owe her an apology, and an explanation of how my distance is my defense mechanism.

"And I told her that she should leave you alone." His shoulders stay straight but I see the uncertainty in his eyes.

"You did what?" I ask, my voice growing unbelievably tight as I give his chest a solid push. Anger is back. Because nothing pushes my buttons like someone messing with my best friend.

I might try to push Ava away, but no one else gets to hurt her.

"I thought—"

"You thought wrong," I snarl. "What did I tell you about being heavy-handed? I don't want it, and I won't tolerate it."

He stops, his jaw working. "I did get heavy-handed again, didn't I?"

My fists clench. "You want a girl that lets you boss her around, go back to your shitty dating app and your sorority girls."

"How did you know…"

"I thought we understood each other. I can be a real bitch, but you will respect my boundaries."

He drops down on his knees, which makes my head whip back, surprise making my eyes wide. "You're right."

"Which part?" I ask, my anger deflating like a balloon.

"All of it. I've pushed too hard and I made choices on your behalf that I shouldn't have made. You're angry. I'm bossy. I need a woman who calls me out on it."

I don't know what he expected, but my hands relax. "Thank goodness."

"What?"

"Is it messed up that it makes me feel better that you're not perfect?" I say shaking my head.

He laughs and then pulls me close, his face settling against my stomach. "You don't think I'm perfect? I think you are."

"Oh please," I snort, but I run my hands through his hair. "We both know I'm as far from perfect as one can get."

He looks up at me then, his eyes open and honest. "You're perfect for me."

My breath catches. "I am not."

"You are, Cadence. I already told you. I don't want simple. I like that you challenge me. I..." His hands spread out on my back. "I'm falling in love with you."

My lips part as I stare down at him. He can't mean it. "Zane." I hear the tears in my own voice.

"You don't have to say it back. I'm still going to help you heal. But I just want you to know that I'm willing to give you my whole heart if you're willing to take it."

I curl around him, my eyes squeezing shut. "I love you too."

"You do?"

"I do. And I want to be the kind of person who knows how to give love and how to receive it."

"Good."

But then I tug on his hair. "But just so we're clear, loving me means taking care of Ava too. I wouldn't be here without her. She's the first person who showed me that some people don't leave. They stay and they love."

He nods. "I'll make my apologies, and from now on…I'm clear. Ava is on the protected list."

I feel like the Grinch, because I swear, I can feel my heart swelling and growing in my chest. What I hoped, what I wanted, has come to pass.

I have found love thanks to The Hunt.

And for the first time in a long time, I think I might be able to work past my anger and live my life with peace and joy.

AND NOW, a sneak peek of the next book in the Kings of Las Vegas series, Ryker's story, King of Corruption!!

# KING OF CORRUPTION

***Until death do us part.***

When my father sells my sister to a cruel Mafia king, I know I need to escape before it's my turn.

I'll need money, so I do the only thing I've ever been good at: counting cards.

From the start, though, I make a huge mistake.

The Las Vegas casino I choose to steal from?

**It belongs to my sister's fiancé.**

I'm hauled into his office, shoved into a chair by his goons as he stands above me, his stare cold enough to freeze my soul.

He's a man who is above the law, he can do anything he wants.

But he does the worst thing of all...he makes me wait. Imagine. Stew.

He'll decide how he wants to punish me *after* the wedding.

I barely pull myself together for the ceremony.

I just have to stand by my sister's side.

Except, my sister is nowhere to be found.

Instead, a white dress hangs on the back of the rectory door.

Turns out, there's been a change of plans.

He's decided on my punishment after all.

And now...

**I'm the bride.**

# KING OF CORRUPTION

Sasha

"How can you allow him to do this to me?" my sister Katarina cries, dropping to her knees at our brother's feet. "How can you let him marry me off like I'm livestock?"

"Livestock does not get *married off*," Dimitri sighs, rubbing his eyes with his forefinger and thumb.

"It gets sold," she fires back, glaring from her spot on the floor. "Just like I am being sold for a casino on the Las Vegas strip."

Dimitri drops his hand. "Technically, the property that Ryker Smith will take over is not on the strip."

"That's supposed to make me feel better?" she cries tossing her hands in the air. "That I'm being traded for an inferior casino?"

"You're not being traded," Dimitri straightens, his eyes hardening. "First and foremost, you will be protected from our father by being married to such a powerful family."

I snort and my brother's glare swings to me. My chin notches in defiance, but I remain silent.

First, because I'm not the one being traded like livestock, but second, it's best if I keep out of my brother's notice for a bit. Katarina and I have an understanding. This is a sinking ship and it's every woman for herself.

"And who will protect me from my new husband?" Katarina's voice rises with every word. "You don't think I haven't heard the whispers about my new family? My future husband? You are tossing me from the frying pan and into the fire!"

I've heard them too. Ryker Smith is known for his ruthless business practices and his uncompromising nature.

I hadn't been in Vegas for ten minutes when stories about his closest brother, Killian Smith, painted a picture. The man stalked his wife, who was desperate for money, and then forced her to marry him.

These are not nice men.

Not that our family is any better. Our father has had us locked in a prison in Russia for the last five years. Now, Katarina is twenty-three, and I'm twenty-one, and we're free from our Russian prison. We're in the United States for one purpose... marry to strengthen our family's business connections.

No, thank you.

I only realize my brother and sister have continued on the conversation without me when Katarina smacks my arm. "Tell him, Sasha."

I give my brother, who is all but a stranger, a blank stare. "Tell him what?"

She lets out a long huff. "Focus, Sasha. Don't crap out on me now."

I wince. There are a few areas that I can focus with absolute and intense concentration. Numbers, for example, just stick in my head.

Conversations about feelings, not so much.

"I'm not crapping out," I frown, my brow creasing. I was just contemplating the likelihood that the Smiths are as ruthlessly narcissistic as our father. They are in the same business. Are willing to arrange marriages for financial gain. They build apartment buildings with the strength of bomb shelters—

"Sasha," Dimitri barks with a scowl. "There are enough opinions in this conversation."

I tell myself to remain silent, but the challenge is more than I can stand. "I don't mind adding mine. I'd say the likelihood is very high that the Smiths are terrible people."

His scowl deepens. "I know them. They are leagues better than our father."

Katarina snorts. "That's not saying much, if it's even true."

Dimitri looks up at the ceiling. "The deal is done. The wedding is happening. And you will be protected under the Smiths' care."

I wrinkle my nose.

Katarina will be protected—at least that's our brother's theory. I'm still in the wind. Not that I'm letting my brother or my father marry me off. I'm not.

I've got my own plan.

All I need is a little cash.

"I won't do it," Katarina cries, her hands clenching into fists. "You can't make me."

Dimitri's glare is so fierce, we both step back. We haven't been allowed access to our brother for seven years, I was still a child the last time I saw him. I don't know this man or what he's capable of.

"I will see you wed to Ryker Smith," he grits through clenched teeth. "It's in your best interest and mine. This conversation is done."

And then he turns, leaving our apartment and slamming the door behind him.

The Smiths, or the Kincaids—I can't keep track of these Las Vegas families—have moved us into a building with top security.

They say it's for our protection. That's what our father said too, but I know a prison when I'm contained in one.

Cameras everywhere, guards at the entrance and exits, elevators that double as vaults. This is a prison.

I draw in a deep breath as Katarina pushes back up to her feet. "Can you believe that?"

"No," I shake my head. "All this time, we thought Dimitri would save us…"

"Seriously," she shakes her head. "He's just as bad as otets."

He is not as bad as our father. Our father would have left a plethora of bruises all over Katarina for her impertinence and might have thrown in a broken arm for good measure.

But there is nothing to be gained by pointing this out. "What will you do?"

"I'm not marrying him." Katarina's chin notches. "I've been a slave long enough."

"How will you get out of the match?" I ask, turning toward her. We look alike. Same dark hair, same brown eyes, same classic features.

But where I'm petite, Katarina is statuesque. And where I'm analytical, Katarina is brimming with emotion.

"Don't worry about that. I'm Russian. I'll come up with something."

Me too. But we're running out of time. The wedding is the day after tomorrow. Once Katarina is married, I'm sure Dimitri will turn his attention to me.

Which means I've got a very narrow window of time in which to enact my plan.

Katarina flounces off to her room, leaving me in the living area. I can give the Smiths credit on one front.

It's a very nice apartment. A luxury kitchen with a large island moves into an eating area, which then flows seamlessly into the living room.

A small hall leads to two bedrooms, each with their own baths.

I walk down the hall, turning right into my bedroom. The slider at the back opens to a balcony, rows of them leading from my third-floor unit to the ground.

That's how I'll escape.

Reaching under my mattress, I pull out a roll of money that I'd carefully concealed for just such an occasion.

My plan is simple. Using my ability to remember numbers, I am going to visit a smaller, less-secure casino, where I'll count the cards and make enough to buy my way out of Vegas.

Thanks to my father, I already had passports and credentials with three different names.

All I need is money.

Simple.

Hopefully.

I take the roll of bills and toss it on the bed as I get ready to change.

I'd never been to one of the Vegas casinos before, but Russian gambling houses had fairly strict dress codes.

I can't wear a gown while shimmying down balconies, but I have a pair of black dress pants that should do the trick.

Pulling them from my drawer, I add a sparkly top and then brush my long brown hair until it shines, before pulling it up into a twist.

Gloss goes on my full lips and dark eyeliner and mascara around my long dark lashes.

In Russia, both Katarina and I were considered beauties.

I don't know about that. But my pink glittering top brings out the color of my cheeks and compliments the brown of my hair.

Satisfied that I won't look like I don't belong, I tuck the money roll into the back of my pants. In a small backpack I pack my passports, a toothbrush and a few pairs of underwear and then sit on the bed, waiting for dark.

Cameras line both the inside and the outside of the building.

I've timed them, of course, learned their schedule as they move back and forth across the side of the building, but I'm going to hedge my bets and wait for dark.

The later it grows, the busier the casino will be, and the easier it will be to blend in with the crowd.

The Vegas sun slowly sinks, painting the sky in hues of orange and red. I like the desert. It has its own beauty that is undeniable.

Too bad I'm not staying.

As the last rays disappear and the sky is shrouded in darkness, I move to the slider, watching the cameras on either corner of the building.

Just as they swing away, I slide open the slider and close it softly again.

Pulling myself over the rail, I shimmy down the bars, dangling down until I get a toe on the rail below. If only I had Katarina's height.

I just get myself balanced on my toe, and then I let go of the balcony above. My back tenses and I nearly fall but just manage to crouch and grab the railing under my feet.

For a second, I just catch my breath. But not for too long, I've got less than thirty seconds before the cameras swing back around.

Repeating the same process, I make it to the first floor. It's easier this time and soon, I'm dropping to the ground.

Sneaking into the bushes that line the building, I wait, letting the cameras sweep back my way.

Softly, I count, timing out the next swing before I dart out of the bushes and into the street.

The air whooshes from my lungs as adrenaline fills my limbs.

I'm free.

For the first time in my entire life, I'm master of my own destiny.

But I'm getting ahead of myself. This is only step one.

Step two is to actually acquire enough money so I can get somewhere that no one will find me.

Not my father. Not my brother. And not my sister's new family.

The Smith brothers can all go to the devil. And Ryker Smith in particular, is a man I don't want to know. I met him once and he made me feel...uncomfortable.

The thought steels my spine, though I know the next part is much harder than the first as I couldn't do much to prepare.

I step out from the side street and onto the strip.

Lights flash, people laughing as they crowd the sidewalks, raising giant cocktails to one another. It's jarring and I shrink away.

I can feel that I don't match their energy, that I'm going to stand out because of it.

I've never been good at putting on a face. Katarina can smile and laugh with a knife at her back, but I can't pretend like that.

I stop at the fountains at the Bellagio as they begin their hourly show, the spray from the water misting my skin. I could go inside, but a place of that quality will have security of the highest caliber.

Knowing that I'm giving off vibes of desperation, I keep walking toward old Vegas, where I'll fit in far better.

The strip is one giant party. Old Vegas is for hard-timers. People who want their drinks without umbrellas and their dinners two-for-one.

The security is also a lot laxer. They are not places for high rollers.

I move past the bachelorette parties and frat gatherings and keep making my way toward Fremont Street.

It's a further walk than I thought and I can feel the sweat dripping down my back, even in the cooler night air.

That's when the Palace comes into view.

Removed from the rest of the new casinos, it's got a different vibe from the new Las Vegas Strip.

For a few seconds, I just stand there, indecision making me rock as I nip at my lip.

Drawing in a breath, I make my choice and cross the street, entering the massive lobby.

It's easy enough to find the casino floor. Cashing in my money, I take my pile of chips and search for a table.

I've decided that five-card poker will be my game. I've been thinking about what sort of dealer I should choose, and I've decided on an older man. Women are shrewd, and older men are frequently protective rather than suspicious of young ladies.

Counting cards is a delicate art, believe it or not. You have to figure out where the deck is at, start keeping track of the cards that have been played, find the rhythm before the deck turns over and gets washed.

You have to have enough money to buy your way through the learning, without arousing suspicion.

I've played poker with my guards since I was a small child, and my memory is flawless.

But the nuance of reading the dealer and keeping the proper temperament, in that I trust myself less.

Still, I choose a dealer who is younger than I hoped, but he's washing a fresh deck. With no automatic shuffler, my job is much easier since there will only be one deck to count.

After watching as many hands as I think I can get away with, I take a seat, doing my best to not look scared out of my mind.

Which isn't really a stretch. But I'm going for innocent-worried rather than guilty-as-hell and frightened-out-of-my-wits.

He deals a single card to each player to determine who has first betting rights and when I'm dealt a king, I know I'm off to a good start.

It doesn't take me long before I win, knowing that the likelihood of the dealer getting the ace he'd need was nearly impossible.

And then I win again. And again.

The dealer goes from smiling to suspicious over the course of four hands, which is my cue to stop.

Collecting up my winnings, I pick a new table.

I'll do one more table, cash in my chips, and move on to another casino.

I pick my mark, watching several hands before I take a seat.

I blow out a breath, the dealer is giving me a weird look. Should I have already left the Palace after one table? Looking around, I swear one of the security guards is eyeing me.

I feel my anxiety rising, a problem I've struggled with my entire life, and so blowing out a breath, I start tapping my fingers into my palm, and then against my legs.

It's an exercise one of the nannies taught me to control my fear and calm my nerves, but it's not working here.

What's more, I watch one of the guards speak into walkie talkie as he looks at me, his gaze taking in my fingers tapping on my legs.

I blink my eyes, and clench my hands into fists, losing focus on the hand and the cards at play.

Still, somehow, I win the hand and then another. I blow out a breath, knowing I need to leave, but I've just gotten a handle on this deck and for the work I put in, I'd like a few more winning hands.

But that is a mistake. I win one more, determined to make the next hand my last at this table, and this casino, when I get a tap on the shoulder.

This is completely different than the tapping I'm unconsciously doing on my knee.

I turn to see a very stern-looking security guard glaring down at me. "Come with me, miss."

My mouth opens and then closes as I do a quick calculation of the chips in front of me. I've barely been here an hour, and I've already made over fifty grand.

It's a lot, but is it really enough to get me in trouble? I start to gather up my chips, but the guard's hand comes to my shoulder. "Leave them," he rumbles gruffly.

"But I won them," I cry, ignoring the shifting of the other gamblers even as the dealer pulls out a fresh deck. "They're mine."

Another guard joins the first, his hand coming to my other shoulder. Cold fear trickles down my spine. "Bag them up," he says to the dealer. "Mister Smith can decide if she gets to keep them or not."

My muscles turn to jelly. "Mister Smith?"

"That's right, girlie. Ryker Smith wants to see you." And then he yanks me up by my upper arm.

My legs don't work, and I start to go down before the other guard grabs my other side and the two of them start dragging me across the casino floor.

If my brain could work, I'd ask myself how I managed to be in one of my sister's fiancé's casinos.

Then again, I should have known. In Vegas, the Smiths are real-estate gods—and criminals besides.

They are above the law, which means that Ryker Smith can do with his thieving little sister-in-law whatever he wishes.

What will he choose? I'm about to find out.

Want to read more? King of Corruption

# LORDS OF LAS VEGAS

The Kings of Las Vegas are part of the Lords of Las Vegas world!
Check out the completed Lords of Las Vegas series!

# MORE ABOUT TAMMY

Tammy is the writer of Bestselling Regency Romance who could not resist the urge of writing in the dark and delicious world of Contemporary Dark and Steamy Billionaire Romance.

She lives with her husband and three children in Massachusetts and her favorite adventures are the ones that are found in books but occasionally she lives a few of her own!

Made in United States
North Haven, CT
11 September 2025

72739476R00135